Billionaire Unloved

THE BILLIONAIRE'S OBESSION

Jett

J. S. SCOTT

Contents

Prologue

Jett

Over Two Years Ago...

"I can't believe you did this to me," my fiancée screamed at me. "I can't marry you like this. I can't even *look* at you, much less have sex with you. You're...disfigured."

Lisette's face was almost purple as she backed away from my hospital bed, an imperfection I knew she'd hate if she knew her face was that color.

Her words hit home, but I was fucking hurting, and it wasn't my *heart* that was causing me excruciating pain. It was my messed-up body and leg that were causing me so much agony that I wished I could be put out of my damn misery.

"I can't have this discussion with you right now, Lisette," I said through gritted teeth.

"There's nothing to discuss. I can't be married to a man who is never going to be able to go to social events and dance with me. Instead of being envious of me, my friends will feel sorry for me because I'm married to somebody who's disabled. I can't stand being pitied. You know I want to be revered. I deserve it," she said with a small huff of displeasure.

Jesus! How had I never noticed what a superficial woman my own fiancée was, or how petty?

Probably because I haven't had much time for anything other than work.

Lisette and I got together for sex and parties.

Generally, I wanted the sex, so I took her wherever she wanted to go.

She hadn't demanded anything more of me than that, and I hadn't needed anything else. Sure, we had talked about setting a date for our wedding, but Lisette had been pretty happy about the expensive diamond I'd put on her finger, and the date hadn't seemed all that important to either one of us. I was starting to think she loved the idea of the expensive ring more than she wanted to be married to me.

Maybe the delay had been a blessing since she was in the process of dumping me while I was still trying to recover from my last surgery.

According to my two brothers, she hadn't been able to come see me earlier because she couldn't tolerate sick people. But she'd run her ass up here in a hurry as soon as I was conscious to break our engagement.

Okay. Yeah. Maybe I'd known that she wasn't *exactly* an intellectual, but I wondered why I'd never realized how narcissistic she was.

Maybe because I'd never done something she didn't approve of before.

I'd never told Lisette about PRO, the volunteer organization that my best friend, Marcus Colter, headed up to rescue kidnapped victims and political prisoners in hostile countries.

Maybe the fact that I'd never trusted her enough to tell her about PRO should have been a big red flag, but I'd told myself that she didn't need to know, and that PRO was a secret group. The team had all kept a low profile.

Honestly, I'd pretty much known that she just didn't give a damn, but I'd never admitted it to myself. Funny what nearly dying will do to a guy. I was thinking about all kinds of shit I never had before.

Strangely, Lisette had never even *asked* how I'd gotten into a helicopter crash in a foreign country. Obviously, the only thing that mattered was how my injuries affected *her*.

"I suppose I should return the ring," she said in a nicer tone.

"Like I said, we can discuss it later."

"I want this over," she said. "I don't want to marry you."

Yeah, I'd pretty much gotten *that* point, but I couldn't say that her words didn't still hurt. I was in a pretty vulnerable position, and the fact that my fiancée couldn't stand to be with me was a bitter pill to swallow right now.

I looked bad. I knew that. When our helicopter had gone down, I'd been on the side that hit the ground, and my whole body was torn up from one end to the other. My leg had gotten mangled, and the doctors were still trying to put it back together.

"Keep the ring," I rasped. All I wanted right now was to suffer in silence without her irritatingly shrill voice lamenting about how I'd ruined everything for her.

Honestly, since I'd been in the accident, I hadn't really thought about how my injuries were going to affect the rest of my life. Hell, I'd just been trying to make it through the day.

I'd been looking forward to finally seeing my fiancée, hoping that she would make me remember how much I had to live for and that I had a future to look forward to.

But I'd been wrong.

Right now, I'd do just about anything to *get rid of her*.

"I think you owe me the diamond after everything you put me through," she mused.

"Other than getting injured, what in the hell did I ever do to you? I bought you *everything* you wanted, exactly when you wanted it. I've sent you on expensive vacations with all of your friends. What else did you want?"

I didn't mention that I'd spent a small fortune on her jewelry collection, and the expensive sports car I'd purchased for her. With Lisette, it was always about material things, but since I could well afford anything she wanted, I'd seen no reason to deny her anything.

"I wanted *you* to stay one of the hottest, richest, most wanted bachelors in the world so that everybody envied me," she said with a pout.

"I'm so fucking sorry that I disappointed you," I answered with cold sarcasm.

All I wanted was for her to get the fuck out of my room.

"Good-bye, Jett," she said dramatically as she sailed out the door.

"Happy trails, bitch," I said aloud after she'd gone.

I looked at the clock and noticed I had another hour before I could get something for pain. It seemed like my whole damn life revolved around my medication schedule.

I tried to relax, but my entire body was tense with pain and irritation.

And *maybe* there was some hurt in there somewhere, too.

The woman I'd thought I loved and was going to spend the rest of my life with had just walked out on me because I was going to be covered with scars and quite honestly, my dancing days *were* over. But I hadn't even contemplated any of those things since I'd just been trying to get through another day staring at the four walls that were beginning to make me feel closed in. But Lisette's harsh comments were beginning to make me think about my future, and it didn't look quite as good as it had before the helicopter crash.

Nothing will ever be the same. I might walk again, but my day-to-day life was going to be different.

I knew that if the positions were reversed, I *never* would have walked away from Lisette. I might be kind of a dick in some ways, but *that* took a meanness that I didn't know existed inside her.

"What in the fuck happened to me?" I grumbled.

When had I *ever* been *okay* with somebody like Lisette, much less been *engaged* to her?

I'd grown up wealthier than most people in the world, but my deceased parents had raised every one of their kids to be decent individuals. My mom and dad had never put money and success before morals and values.

I wondered what else I'd been ignoring while I'd been wrapped up in growing one of the biggest tech companies in the world with my brothers Mason and Carter.

Somehow, if I ever got out of this damn hospital and out of the pain that was tearing my wounded body apart, I was going to pay attention to what was happening in the world around me again. And I was never fucking letting myself get sucked in by a woman who had no substance because I was *busy.*

The engagement had been Lisette's idea, and I'd felt like I owed her the respect of giving her a ring since we'd been dating for over a year. It just seemed like a natural progression, and I wasn't averse to being married. And since I'd never seen her nasty side, I thought we'd be happy together.

Now, I was doubting the decisions I'd made while my brothers and I were trying to send our company into the stratosphere. I had to wonder where the hell my brain and my heart had been while I was working twelve hour days in my office. We'd achieved our goal, but at what price? I'd almost married a woman with no heart.

I'll find somebody someday who doesn't care that my body has a considerable number of scars, and that I can't dance.

The prognosis on my leg wasn't good. I'd need more surgeries, and even after they were done, I'd never have the same mobility I'd had before the accident.

In my world, finding a woman who'd accept my appearance and limitations was highly unlikely. If they did, they'd be in it for the money.

Since I'd been born wealthy, I knew how superficial my world could be sometimes. Maybe *that* was my motivation to be part of Marcus's team. I wanted to make some kind of difference in the world, and not by donating money that was tax deductible.

Now that I'd had my come-to-Jesus moment, I knew I was never going to go down the same road as I'd been on most of my adult life.

Life was finite, and nobody knew that more than a guy who had cheated death.

I had no idea if there was a woman who could see more than my money when she looked at me. A woman who thought scars and a bum leg were no big deal. But if I did run into her somewhere, I sure as hell wouldn't let her get away. I'd ask her to marry me on the spot.

If I *didn't* meet her, I was better off alone.

Chapter 1

Ruby

The Present...

I felt like my whole crappy life had led to the nightmare I was currently experiencing.

I was naked.

There was a chain around my waist that my captor was pulling on to propel me forward. Unfortunately, the guy pulling my chain—literally—was a whole lot bigger and heavier than I was, so I was forced to keep moving.

And in a matter of moments, I knew I'd be standing on a stage with plenty of buyers staring at my nude body and trying to decide how much money me *and* my virginity was worth to them.

My fight-or-flight instincts were screaming at me to escape. *Flight* would be my *only* option because I'd never been much of a fighter.

For me, resistance had always meant *more pain*. After the first few lessons as a child, I'd learned not to fight anymore because it didn't gain me anything.

At least, it never had until now, but old habits and programmed behavior weren't going to go away.

However, my panic was making me think I might have to change in a hurry.

I have to get the hell out of here!

I hated the fact that I'd gotten myself into this position because of my own stupidity, but regret wasn't going to improve my situation. I was going to have to find a way to escape or suffer the consequences.

How had I ever fallen for my kidnapper's story?

I'd been homeless and desperate when my abductors had offered me a job. Hunger had been a good motivator since I'd ended up accepting the offer because I hadn't eaten in days.

Because of my bad decision, I hadn't seen the light of day since I'd gotten into their car that day a few weeks ago. I'd been held in a bug-infested hotel room with barred windows and no chance of escape.

The only *good* thing about my makeshift prison had been the food. I'd been fed, but the meals hadn't been given out of kindness or to build my strength to work an actual job. My kidnappers had wanted to fatten me up like a farmer wants to put weight on their cattle to make them more attractive to buyers.

My body was shaking as I was led onto the stage. I wasn't terrified about being naked, which, in itself, would generally be terrifying. But I had more dire things to worry about, like *who* was going to bid high enough in this crazy virgin auction to own me, and what their plan for me might be *after* the sale.

Would I end up chained in the dirt in the darkness of a cellar or basement, never to be seen again?

Maybe there was no one who cared about me in this world, but I sure as hell didn't want that fate.

I flinched as I was pulled into place on the stage and kept there by the man holding the chain.

The humiliation of being leered at by a crowd of men hit me like a powerful slam in the stomach.

I'd lived with humiliation all my life, and for a few seconds, I flashed back to some of those memories, something I *never* allowed myself to do. But my terror was out of control, and I had no way to defend myself or to make those images escape my brain.

I couldn't see every pair of eyes watching me. But I felt the creepy sensation of being watched by many sets of eyes, and it made me want to drop into a fetal position to protect myself.

Don't panic. Dani said she was going to rescue me.

The problem was, I didn't really *know* Danica Lawson well enough to judge whether somebody *would* come to help me. But her promise was about the only thing I had to keep me going. We'd only met once in person, and talked on the phone a few times. She'd seemed nice enough, but I'd learned early in life that people let me down, and that the only one who really cared about my survival was *me.*

I lifted my chin, determined not to let anybody know how scared I was. I'd been through bad situations before, and I refused to cower to these people who degraded women for entertainment. Some people got off on humiliating others, and I wasn't about to give any potential buyers reason to pay more for a woman who would tremble and cry at their feet.

One thing I didn't do was cry, even when I desperately needed that relief.

Crying gave tormentors power, and I refused to let go of what little dignity I still had left.

I'll find a way to escape if Dani doesn't come.

Getting free was my only hope, and because I was fed and rested, I was a hell of a lot stronger than I'd been when I'd been captured.

I tried to relax enough to get me to another place, to let my mind lead me to anywhere else but where I was at the moment. It was a childhood trick I'd adopted when I didn't want to be aware of what was happening to me because it was too damn painful.

I tried, but I soon realized that escaping inside myself wasn't going to work this time. So I stared into the sea of faces I could make out in the smoke-filled room.

The lights on the stage were bright enough that I couldn't see much except the people closest to me in the first row or two of tables. My eyes moved and landed on one face, and for some reason, I couldn't look away.

My rapidly beating heart tripped as I stared at the man in the front row.

For an instant, I felt comforted as he looked into my eyes, seemingly ignoring the fact that I was naked. Were his eyes trying to say something to me, or was I imagining it because I wanted to think he felt some kind of compassion for me?

As the auctioneer started to talk about the many ways I could be used and abused if I was sold to someone with darker fetishes, I broke eye contact with the dark-haired man.

There's no kindness for me. It was obviously just a desperate thought. Nobody with a heart could sit and watch women get auctioned off like farm animals.

A moment later, I knew I was right when the man I'd hoped wasn't looking at my body but was seeing *me* actually placed his own bid.

Nobody here cares about me. All they want is my body to use and abuse.

I blinked back tears as I continued to stare into the darkness at the back of the room, my body rigid even though all I wanted to do was collapse on the floor in a puddle of hopelessness.

I don't cry. I never cry. I won't give anybody here the satisfaction of knowing I'm terrified.

In a moment of weakness, I wished that I had mustered up the courage to somehow kill myself to avoid the humiliation that was washing over me in painful waves. Maybe I could have found a way to die, but my will to survive was stronger than my desire to sink into the oblivion of death.

I shook off the dark thought, knowing I'd never willingly give up my life, even though I felt like any hope of ever truly living had left me a long time ago.

I'll get free. I'll find a way.

I remembered a quote I'd read that was connected to Roosevelt: *If you have reached the end of your rope, tie a knot and hang on.*

I was clinging to *my knot* right now, a glimmer of hope I'd never been able to let go of, and I refused to release it.

I'd been inspired by quotes and literature all my life. Since the library was available to everyone, I'd spent most of my time there absorbing as much information and inspiration I could find between the pages of books and other information provided to the public for free.

In my youth, books had been my escape, my way of leaving my painful life behind for short periods of time.

As a homeless adult, it had been a place to stay warm or to cool off, a location that had always found me a place to belong and fit in. Even if it was only for a little while.

Unfortunately, there were no fairy tales for me to fall into right now.

Sold!!!

That one word barked by the auctioneer jolted me back from my musings and into the position that was now my reality: naked, terrified, and on a stage in front of people who wanted to do me harm.

I'd just been sold like a horse at auction, and my reins were about to change hands.

My eyes darted around the room in horror, trying to find my way out.

I pushed my long brown hair back with a trembling hand. My price had gone over six figures, so even if I escaped, I knew I'd be hunted down like an escaped convict. *Nobody* was going to pay that much money and lose an expensive brood mare.

But I knew I'd rather make a break for freedom and be on the run than to just accept whatever my fate was going to be.

I watched as my purchaser went to the cashier to arrange payment while I was pulled down the steps and out of the bright lights that had nearly blinded me.

We came to a stop beside the man who had bought me, and disappointment nearly crushed me as I realized my new owner was the very man who had given me momentary hope.

It was the dark-haired guy from the front row who had briefly met my eyes with what I'd perceived as kindness.

As usual, I'd been so damn wrong.

I blinked as he looked up at me, his expression now filled with anger.

"Cover her and release her!" he barked at the man still holding my chain.

My restraint was removed, and I was handed a dark cover-up that I quickly donned. It was thin, like something a woman would wear to cover a bathing suit, but I gladly pulled the material down over my privates, relieved that I could cover my body.

"Let's go," my new nemesis growled into my ear as he took my upper arm to guide me out of the club.

His grip was insistent and firm, but not painfully so.

I moved with him, anxious to get out of a club that was sleazy enough to auction off virgins, not caring whether the women were there willingly or unwillingly.

I had a feeling that nearly every woman being sold was completely unwilling, or had been forced to be here by tragedy.

I'd met two women in the holding area who had been sold off to somebody in a third world country. They'd been tourists in the US for a holiday, normal sightseers in a country that was the land of the free. I'm sure it had rightly never crossed their minds that they'd become victims of a kidnapping, and now it was entirely possible that they might never see their home countries again.

The two travelers had people who loved them back home, and I desperately wanted to help them. But I couldn't do it as a prisoner.

I stumbled slightly to keep up with the man who now owned me. He wasn't moving that fast, but my feet were bare. I occasionally stepped on what I assumed were peanut shells, but I was pretty sure I didn't really want to know if it was anything else.

That's when I noticed that my latest captor had a weakness, a slight limp to his step that I could probably use to my advantage. It wasn't much, but considering his massive size and strength, I'd take whatever help I could get.

My heart nearly exploded with relief as I realized that I could probably outrun him if I could just get outside.

He pushed through the heavy wooden doors with a powerful arm, and I welcomed the humid air that suddenly enfolded me.

I took a deep breath, and ended up gasping, trying to suck up the outside air after being in a putrid environment for so long.

My escort released my arm as he motioned toward the parking lot to indicate that he was parked beside the building.

I was scared, but another quote floated into my mind:

Freedom lies in being bold!

I was pretty sure the great poet Robert Frost was responsible for writing that phrase, but I was too terrified to be certain. All I knew was that those words were completely true in my situation.

I had to have courage if I was going to live.

My buyer stepped forward to make his way to the parking lot.

And I took off like a shot in the opposite direction.

"Ruby!" I heard the irritated male bellow, but I didn't stop.

I was pretty much determined to escape…or die trying.

Chapter 2

Ruby

I t didn't take me long to realize that I was in one of the roughest parts of Miami, but I didn't care. My bare feet kept hitting the pavement, and I told myself I'd rather face the seedy area than to give in to a man who had paid a fortune to own me.

Once I was outside the lights of the club, I was met by darkness. Most of the businesses were closed, and the light was so dim that I couldn't see where I was going.

But I kept running until I could hear my own ragged breath as I kept pushing forward, getting so close to freedom that I could almost taste it.

Certainly, my nemesis would have to stop because of his bum leg, and if I could just keep going, I knew I could outlast his endurance.

I had far more at stake than he did.

I was out of breath, and in bad shape from the weeks I'd been held captive and inactive, but my drive and energy was strong from being well-fed and terrified.

Please, just let me escape.

My fear kept my legs moving, but the lack of light caused my leg to come down on something that sent excruciating pain shooting through my foot.

"Ouch!" I cried out, trying not to let my injury stop me.

My steps faltered as the agony gave way to hopelessness. I knew the slowdown was going to put me at risk.

I tried to keep moving, but I would have fallen if a powerful body hadn't slammed into my back, and supporting arms hadn't wrapped around me.

"Noooo!" I howled, knowing my escape had been brief and the price would probably be pretty damn high.

I couldn't see *him* since he was behind me, but I knew that my buyer had successfully hunted down his expensive purchase.

Whatever advantages I'd had were lost.

As I struggled to get out of his strong hold, I could hear his harsh breath on the side of my neck. His grip wasn't cruel, but he made it clear that he was hanging onto what was now his property.

Me!

"Just let me go," I cried out desperately.

I gave in to the despair that had been hanging over me for weeks like a dark cloud, the pain of the injury to my foot exacerbating the feeling of helplessness that I'd come to hate.

His voice was harsh as he rasped, "I'm not here to hurt you, woman. I'm here to help. Dani sent me."

My panicked brain took a moment to acknowledge what he said. *My new friend had sent me help? She'd really come through?*

"Who are you?" I asked, my throat balking at the usage of my voice after my marathon sprint.

His hold on me relaxed as he answered gruffly, "My name is Jett. I'm Dani's brother. She sent me here to rescue you. I'm sorry you had to be afraid during the auction. It seemed easier to buy your freedom than to take on people who might hurt you, and I'm solo on this gig."

Freedom? I hardly knew what that meant anymore, but I wanted it more than I'd ever wanted anything. I'd never truly been *free*.

I opened my mouth, but a sob was ready to escape, so I immediately shut it down.

I'm not going to cry. I refuse to cry.

Maybe Jett was the good guy, but I was horribly afraid that if I started to cry, I'd never stop.

Relief flowed over me, and the only thing that kept me standing was Jett's hold on me as he turned me around and surprisingly wrapped his arms around me.

I felt more secure than I ever had in my twenty-two years of existence on Earth.

I wasn't sure exactly why, but I was pretty certain it had something to do with the strength and power that he seemed to exude from every pore in his body.

He didn't speak as I wrapped my arms around his neck and panted against his shoulder. His hands stroked over my hair and down my back, his touch comforting.

"It's over, Ruby. I promise you, it's over." Jett's voice was husky and deep as he made a vow with so much certainty that it made me feel even safer, more secure.

And feeling protected wasn't something I'd ever experienced in my past.

I was calmer as I finally answered, "But now I'm indebted to you," I pointed out in a tremulous voice. "You just shelled out a fortune."

Jett had paid more money for me than I could even process in my mind. I felt rich when I had enough money to buy a hamburger from the dollar menu, so figures like he'd just given to gain my freedom were incomprehensible to me.

"Don't worry about the money," he rasped. "Let's just get you somewhere safe."

He wrapped his arm around my waist, but I still winced as I tried to put more weight on my foot. "I have to go slow," I said as all the breath *whooshed* out of my lungs from the pain of trying to walk.

"What happened?" he asked brusquely as he stooped down to try to look at my injury.

"I think I stepped on something," I answered.

A small beam of light illuminated my lower extremities and I heard Jett curse. "Fuck! You're bleeding all over the sidewalk. I can feel the blood."

He had his cell phone in his hand, and he used the light to look back at the large pieces of glass behind us. "You didn't just step on *something*," he said. "It looks like a damn massacre. You ran through shards of glass."

"I can make it to the car," I said shakily. I just wanted to get out of the general area of the club.

"Damn right you will," Jett grumbled as he handed me the cell phone that provided light and hefted me into his arms before I could protest.

He limped heavily as he took on my weight, but his long strides had us both in his car within a short period of time.

I felt horrible because I knew Jett had to be hurting, but I hadn't heard a single word of complaint come out of his mouth. And it would have caused him more grief if I'd struggled to get down.

I heaved a sigh as he got behind the wheel after wrapping my foot with his own T-shirt.

I didn't see his scars until he was seated, the overhead lights illuminating his body and face.

Very little could have marred the masculine beauty of his face. He had one or two small scars at his temple that looked like they'd faded over time, but Jett was so in-your-face gorgeous that a few little marks didn't matter. As my eyes took in his powerful chest and torso, I could see he'd been in a horrible accident at one time.

Somehow, it was comforting that we were both survivors. Not that I wished Jett pain of any kind, but I felt a kinship toward the man who was my rescuer.

Pain is personal. It really belongs to the one feeling it.

I'd read that somewhere, and at the time, I'd really believed it to be true. The words had stuck in my brain.

But now I could actually empathize with my rescuer.

Jett's scars were external.

Mine were all over my soul.

We'd obviously both experienced our share of pain.

My gaze moved up again, and I met his gorgeous green-eyed stare as he turned his head to look at me. "I'm sorry you have to look at my scarred-up body. But you needed my shirt," he said gruffly.

I shrugged. Jett was breathtaking, even *with* all his scars. "You look fine without it. But I'm sorry I ruined it."

He looked taken aback, and then he scowled as he shut off the light and started the car.

He put the vehicle into motion, and I wondered, after the fact, if Jett thought he needed to hide his body just because he had a few imperfections.

I wanted to ask him, but I stayed mute. He'd been nice to me, but he was an intimidating guy because of his size and generally unhappy expression. He didn't know me well enough to *trust me*, and he didn't appear to be very *trusting*. Like me, he looked the type of man who didn't trust anybody but himself.

I'd *tried* to trust the couple who had kidnapped me because I was desperate for food. *And look how that had turned out.*

I was grateful that Jett had rescued me, and I'd do everything in my power to pay him back one day, but I just wasn't willing to put my faith in anybody.

It had always been safer that way.

Chapter 3

Ruby

A few hours later, I listened as the emergency room doctor put a brace on Jett's knee, trying to hear what the verdict would be on his injured leg. Unfortunately, the physician had pulled the curtain between our ER beds, so I couldn't really *see* what was happening.

Thinking we were a couple when we'd come through the door, the nurse had put us into a room that had two beds. Jett had talked me through my x-rays and the extensive number of stitches I'd needed to repair the gash on my foot.

My wound would heal pretty quickly.

But I wasn't sure about Jett's knee.

I was riddled with guilt over the fact that he'd been injured, and I hadn't even known there was anything wrong with Jett until the nurse had mentioned how badly his knee was swelling. I'd been mortified when I saw how the denim of his jeans was stretched because his knee was the size of a grapefruit. The nurse had insisted he get checked out, too, something I'd be eternally grateful for since I hadn't seen the damage myself.

I'd been too busy worrying about my own injuries, and I hated hospitals, not because I'd spent much time in them, but due to the one horrifying experience I'd had with the institution.

I'd been so distracted with trying to keep myself calm that I'd failed to notice that Jett's knee was injured.

He'd just gotten back from his MRI a few minutes ago, and he'd blown the whole thing off by saying he'd had much worse injuries in his life.

However, I hadn't *caused* any of his *other* injuries, but I felt directly responsible for the sprint he'd had to do earlier to catch up to me. And I cringed every time I thought about him picking up my weight so effortlessly and carrying me to his car.

My ears perked up like an alert dog's as the doctor started to speak.

"Rest, ice, the brace, and keep it elevated to get the swelling down," the doctor said in a voice loud enough for me to hear. "Your meniscus is torn, but the tear is in an area that gets good blood flow, so if you do what you're supposed to do, it should eventually heal. Physical therapy—"

Jett interrupted in a cranky tone, "I know the drill, Doc. No sense wasting your breath on my injury. I've had more PT than any person should ever have to have in their lifetime. I go through the routines myself at home now."

"I can see that that you've had a long road with this leg," the doctor said in a more sympathetic voice.

"My knee was already a mess anyway," Jett said flatly. "Whatever I did to it tonight is no big deal."

"It *has* taken a beating," the doctor agreed. "But you didn't have to add another injury. No more sprints for you in the near future. You'll need to be re-checked, and your orthopedic doctor in Seattle wants to see you once you're back home so he can see how you're healing."

"Got it," Jett grumbled.

I had to hold back a squeak of surprise as the curtain was suddenly jerked open, and I could see Jett's unhappy face staring at the doctor like he wanted to punch him.

"The nurse will bring all your discharge instructions shortly," the doctor said right before he exited and pulled the door closed behind him.

The room was silent for a moment before I finally said, "I'm sorry. I'm so sorry."

"It's nothing, Ruby. Don't worry about it. I've had far worse injuries than this one," he answered in an annoyed tone.

Somehow, I knew he wasn't irritated with me, but he should be.

"I didn't *cause* your other injuries," I replied, my voice heavy with regret. "This is my fault. I shouldn't have run away, and there's no way you should have been carrying me."

"Enough!" he said in a booming tone. "I might have scars, and my leg isn't the greatest, but I'm not a fucking invalid. The last thing I need is to be treated like I need to hang it up just because I have a leg that doesn't always cooperate."

I was a little scared of the volume of his voice, but if I looked at things logically, I could see that he was more frustrated than angry.

He sat up with a blanket still covering his legs as he continued in a calmer tone, "You didn't *cause* this, Ruby. In case you didn't notice in the car, I had some pretty severe injuries from a helicopter crash a few years ago. I've been doing workouts every day to strengthen my quads so they supported my bad knee better, but it was always going to be weak and prone to injury. I'll heal."

"You shouldn't have come after me," I said in a tearful voice as I sat up and was finally able to look him directly in the eyes.

I won't cry. I'm not going to cry.

We were both still in hospital gowns, and we were staring each other down. I might have seen the humor in having a hospital argument if I didn't feel so crappy about what had happened.

"There was never any question about whether or not I was going to find you after you bolted," he growled. "We were in a shitty area of Miami, and you were almost naked. I wasn't going to leave you after I'd just gotten you out of harm's way."

My chest ached from his words. "Most people would have," I said in a voice that was almost a whisper. "But I guess *most people* wouldn't have tried to help me in the first place."

I dropped my head and we lost eye contact. Jett was intense, and I wasn't quite sure how to deal with a guy like him. What kind of person tears after somebody who's in trouble with no consideration about injuring themselves? Not anybody I'd ever known.

I was intimidated by guys who were bigger and louder than I was, but I'd also learned that actions meant more than words. And Jett had been there when nobody else *could* or *would* have been.

Problem was, I just didn't understand him at all.

Who, in their right mind, goes off and rescues a woman he doesn't even know? I couldn't even call his sister a real friend since we'd just met a few months ago. But these people, *this family*, had made it their business to help me out.

"How do I ever repay you and Dani for what you did for me?" I asked as I looked down at the tile floor. "How can I ever make up for getting you injured?"

I wasn't used to anybody helping me, so I was at a loss on how to deal with all of this.

My question had pretty much been senseless because I could *never* pay him back anytime soon for the funds he'd shoveled out, or for the injury he'd taken on because of me.

"You can give the police your statement and then testify to put down the organization that profits off human trafficking," he answered. "The people who kidnapped you were minions, part of a far more powerful group that operates all over the world. You can help put them out of business for good."

I shook my head, still unable to meet his gaze as I said, "Who is going to believe me? I'm a homeless woman with no real family. I'm a nobody. I always have been. And I'm sure the top guy is probably rich."

"He is. He's well regarded in this city because he has money and donates to charity to keep his cover," Jett said irritably.

"Then they'll *never* believe me," I said in a shaky voice.

Out of the corner of my eye, I saw Jett moving, but I was still startled as he put his fingers on my chin and forced it upward until our gazes locked.

His green eyes grew stormy as he looked at me. "I know it won't be easy," he said in a kinder tone. "But I'll be there to give my statement about what happened, too, and I'll testify. The money I paid can easily be tracked. These people need to go to jail, Ruby. The couple who kidnapped you should be behind bars where they can't hurt any more women ever again."

"I'll try," I agreed.

I *wanted* everybody involved in the human trafficking ring to be unable to hurt anybody else. I didn't want to see *any* woman to go through what I had.

But I was afraid because my word held no weight. I'd experienced the sense of being invisible to most people the whole time I'd been homeless. "I'm just not sure they'll believe me."

"You're brave, Ruby. You can do it," Jett encouraged in a persuasive baritone that left little room for argument.

"*Necessity makes even the timid brave,*" I mumbled.

"Isn't that Sallust?" Jett questioned. "You're into Roman history?"

I sighed. "I spend a lot of time in the library. I read a lot of things that come back to me at the weirdest of times."

I didn't tell him that I really used those little bits of knowledge to stay connected to the real world. If I was still learning, then I still existed.

His eyes bored into mine as he replied, "I don't think you're timid. I think you're just afraid. And since life has basically shit on you, I can't say I blame you."

I stared back at him and replied, "You'd be surprised." I'd learned to be submissive because being any other way was more painful.

He took my hand in his, and I didn't balk because it felt so good to be connected to someone. I wanted to pull away instinctively, but I liked the false sense of security too much.

"Could you live with yourself if you don't try?" he asked.

B. A. Scott

"It isn't that I don't want to," I explained in a rush. "I do. But because I'm some homeless nobody, they aren't likely to believe me. They'll think I'm delusional."

Because many of the people who had no place to go were mentally ill, it was the common assumption. But in reality, people were on the streets for various reasons. We all had a story, and most of them had very bad endings.

I was merely nonexistent to most people, an unfortunate woman who people assumed was a drug addict, an alcoholic, or mentally ill when I was seen sleeping in a public place. The world seemed like it evolved around me while I was always in the same place.

"I have a solution," Jett said in a guttural voice.

I was falling into his beautiful green eyes, temporarily mesmerized by the determination I could see in the depths of his stare. "What?" I murmured.

"Do you really want to pay me back?" he asked.

"Yes!" I said immediately.

Just ask me. I'll do whatever you want.

Having sex with him wasn't altogether unappealing, even though I had my doubts whether he'd really want a skinny homeless woman who hadn't been able to do anything about her straggly hair, torn up nails, bad skin, or anything else that resembled self-care for years.

"Marry me," he said in a husky tone that was a demand and not a question.

"What?" I was certain I'd misheard him during my temporary stupor.

"Marry. Me."

My eyes widened as I realized I'd heard him correctly. "What?"

"Think about it, Ruby. I'm a well-known technical guy in my field. I have my own company and I'm a businessman. Nobody would ever know how we met, or why we'd married once it comes time to testify. You'd be my wife, and unless you have a criminal history, your background wouldn't even be in question. I'd find a way to make sure it never even comes up."

"I-I've never been in trouble," I stammered. "To most people, I just don't exist."

"You'd have a home address, and a life nobody would bother to investigate since you're just a witness."

"I don't really know what it's like to have a real home," I blurted out, my tone wistful.

"You'll have one if you marry me," he vowed. "You'll never see another day on the streets again. I promise."

My heart skittered as I looked at his sincere expression.

I was a realist, but the deeply buried hope inside me desperately wanted to say *yes* to Jett's insane proposal.

I had very little to lose.

"I'd get so much, and you'd get so little," I said breathlessly. "You'd be saddled with a woman who had been homeless her entire adult life."

"I'd get *a lot*. I'd get *you*," he answered simply. "And if you're unhappy with the arrangement after your testimony, we'll get the marriage annulled."

So he's not expecting to have sex if he's talking about getting the marriage annulled. What is his motive then?

As crazy as it was, I actually *was* tempted. Would life be any worse as somebody's wife than it was on the streets?

I'd be warm at night.

I'd have a roof over my head.

And if I was lucky, I'd have food to eat every day.

The only thing that stopped me from saying *yes* was the fact that Jett was getting far less from the deal than I would.

"I *want* you to say *yes*, Ruby," Jett prompted as he cupped my face with his hands.

I nearly melted at the sensation of his touch. For a big guy with a cranky attitude, he was surprisingly gentle.

There was only silence as I debated what to say to him.

Honestly, I felt like I was in the middle of a dream, and nobody had kicked the park bench yet.

I didn't understand his motivation, but I still desperately wanted to take a chance.

Was the proposal fair to Jett?

But then, he *was* the one who had brought up the idea, so he had to have his reasons for wanting the arrangement, right?

Could I really marry a guy I didn't even know?

Confused, jumbled thoughts continued to run through my brain until I finally made my decision.

I broke eye contact with him as I muttered my answer in a barely audible voice, certain that it was the only answer I could give him.

But for some reason, that single word that had come out of my mouth had somehow felt so very wrong that I didn't look at Jett again as the nurse entered the room with our discharge instructions and we were ready to leave the hospital.

Chapter 4

Ruby

A few weeks later, I *did* regret the fact that I hadn't become Jett Lawson's wife.

Well…for *me* anyway.

For *Jett*…it had been the right call.

I'd learned a few things about Jett Lawson over the past few weeks:

Number one, he was stubborn and he definitely liked to get his own way, but not in a selfish kind of manner. He was usually looking out for somebody else when he got bossy. Lately, that *somebody* had been me.

Number two, he worked a lot. When we were at Marcus's condo, Jett was almost always deep into his computer work with a laser focus that I wished I had.

Number three, I'd hurt him when I'd refused his marriage proposal. As hard as it was for me to accept, his offer had been sincere, and ever since I'd refused him, he'd been reserved and distant.

I knew I had done the right thing when I'd given him my *no* answer at the hospital.

For me, the marriage would have been the one lucky thing that had happened in my otherwise nightmarish life.

For Jett, making me his wife would be an act of kindness.

So while I regretted the fact that I wasn't going to be married to the man who had been so good to me since the day we met. I knew he didn't deserve a homeless woman with no decent future in sight.

Unfortunately for me, I still had a childhood fairy tale in my head that said that a couple should be in love when they get married. And although I'd gladly take a marriage of convenience and friendship opposed to the miserable life I had now, Jett should be looking for a whole lot more.

He'd felt sorry for me.

And pity was no basis for marriage.

Jett had gotten me through giving my statements to the police and the FBI interviews that followed by claiming me as his girlfriend, and giving me his home address and information. So even though we weren't married, I was under his protection when it came to my fears of being ignored or disregarded.

The kingpin of the human trafficking organization had been taken down by Jett's sister, Dani, so all that was left for us to do was to testify against our kidnappers and we were currently waiting to find out more about when that would happen and how everything was going to work out for indictments.

"Are you okay?" Jett asked gruffly from across the small table of the restaurant he'd chosen for dinner.

I realized I'd been staring at the wall, lost in my own thoughts as I answered, "Yeah. I'm good."

"Is this about the stuff I picked up for you? Because if it is, we can exchange anything you don't like."

Oh yeah, there *was* a *number four*. Jett Lawson seemed to think it was his duty to get me everything I didn't have.

I knew from our conversations that Jett had a good job, but I had no idea how much he made as a tech guy who owned his own business.

Obviously, he'd had enough money or credit to pay over a hundred grand to buy my freedom. But by freeing me, Jett could have completely cleaned out his savings and credit lines. And I worried about that since I didn't have a job or a place to live, so I couldn't get that money back to him anytime soon.

"Every single thing you got was top of the line. How could I *not* like that stuff? But I *don't* like the fact that you're spending money on me."

Jett had gone way overboard on buying me what he considered *necessities*.

Once he'd found out what size I wore when we'd made a stop to buy me jeans and shirts, he'd ended producing a whole wardrobe for me a few days later.

New things came every single day to Marcus's condo, and my guilt was pretty much choking me. Jett and I were using Marcus's place until we were done with all of the FBI questioning and interviews, so at least he wasn't paying for our stay. But what he saved wasn't nearly the same amount as the items he was buying.

We'd had several discussions about his over-the-top tendencies when it came to getting things he thought I needed. But I usually felt like I was talking to a brick wall.

Today, I'd gotten the latest and greatest cell phone on the market, and a laptop. I'd cringed at the amount of money it had cost him.

He shrugged as he set his menu aside. "The stuff didn't exactly break me."

Relieved, I smiled back at him. "I really would have been okay with just a few pair of jeans. I didn't need anything else."

Just having an extra set or two of clothes was a big deal for me. I'd end up back on the streets once Jett left, a place where anything except food and clothing just weren't all that important.

He shook his head. "I wouldn't have been good with that," he said.

As usual, his comment was vague, with no explanation as to why he felt he needed to give me things that I'd never be able to carry with me once I was homeless again.

In between buying me things he thought I needed, Jett had managed to track down the two women who had been held captive with me at the club, and he'd learned that they had both escaped and were safely back in their home countries.

Finding the other women who had been victims of the sex trafficking enterprise had been only one of the many things I'd seen him do that told me he was a decent guy.

Okay, maybe more than just *decent*. To me, Jett was *extraordinary*, no matter how much he grumbled.

The waiter arrived to take our order. After he retreated, I asked Jett, "How old are you?"

Okay. Yeah. It *was* weird that I didn't even know the basics about the guy I'd been staying with for weeks, but I *wanted* to know more. I just wasn't feeling his willingness to be open with me, so maybe I was going to have to be the one who pushed.

"I just turned thirty-one last month," he answered.

"Is Dani older or younger?"

He leaned back in his chair and looked at me. "She's the baby of the family. There's five of us. Harper, my other sister, is between me and Dani. And I have two older brothers."

I took a cautious sip of the glass of wine the waiter had just delivered before I replied, "I wish I had siblings."

He raised an eyebrow. "So I take it you don't?"

I knew Jett would like to know more about why I was on the streets, but he hadn't asked me anything personal until now.

I shook my head slowly. "I don't have anyone."

His face turned grim, and he looked like he wanted to say something, but he seemed to shake it off and reached for his drink.

"I'd like the chance to thank your sister for what she did," I said softly. "We barely knew each other, yet she was willing to send you to help me when she was rushing into her own bad situation."

Jett had mentioned some of Dani's history, and what she'd been doing in Florida. I'd been pretty surprised when I'd discover that she was trying to take down a millionaire who was completely corrupt and the ringleader of not only the sex trafficking operation, but a lot of other despicable crimes.

He shrugged. "I guess you have to know Dani. She's always had a big heart."

"And your other sister?"

"She's the same way," he admitted.

"And your parents?" I asked, feeling like I was tugging information from him, little by little.

He shook his head, his expression grim. "They were both killed in a car accident. But they were both incredible."

So are you.

Jett Lawson obviously had the same qualities when it came to helping other people as his sisters did, even though he *tried* to blow it off as nothing.

Since I hated the sudden sadness I saw in his extraordinary eyes, I changed the subject. "So will you be going back to Seattle soon?"

I started to fumble with my linen napkin, waiting uneasily to get his answer.

"Pretty soon," he said noncommittally. "When I do, you're coming with me."

My heart tripped at the thought of staying with Jett, but I knew I couldn't hang out as a guest of his forever. He'd already done way too much for me. "For how long?"

"Do we really need to set a time limit on friendship?" he asked.

Were Jett and I really friends? Mostly, he'd pretty much been stuck with me because he was too nice to dump me back on the streets.

I shook my head slowly. "No. Friendship shouldn't have a time limit. But I'm...scared."

"Of me?" he asked, glancing up to look at me as he waited for an answer with a disappointed expression.

"No," I said immediately. "I'm not afraid *of* you. But I'm terrified that I'll get too used to being with you, too used to sleeping in a real bed, and much too used to not being alone."

Becoming accustomed to something that was going to eventually end was never a good idea.

"You're *never* going to be alone again, and you need to get that into your head right now," Jett rumbled. "Do you honestly think I'm *ever* going to put you out on the streets? It's not going to happen, Ruby. I don't care if it takes *years* for you to get into a position to be on your own. Until that happens, you stay with me, or you let me get you a place here in Florida and pay your bills until you can make it on your own. Those are your choices."

I balked at his bossiness, but I shoved my indignation away as quickly as it appeared. Really, I wanted some kind of normal life so badly I could almost taste it. I longed for a stability I'd never experienced. Someday, I wanted to repay Jett for every cent he'd spent on me. It might take decades to return the money he'd spent to get me off the auction block and to somewhere safe, but I *would* pay him back.

The FBI had told Jett that he might be able to recover some or all of his money, but it could take years, and there was no guarantee he'd ever see a penny of the funds he paid out. Everything would depend on where the finances of the ringleader ended up after the investigation was over.

Tears sprang to my eyes as I told him, "You've already done way too much for somebody you don't even know. I already owe you so much."

"You don't *owe me* a damn thing," Jett said in a low, growly tone.

I stared at him, astonished that he'd even say something like that. "You and I both know that isn't true."

"You really want to repay me?" he said in a demanding voice.

"You know I do."

"Then come to Seattle with me. Stay with me and be my assistant. I've had to do the majority of my work at my home office because of my accident, and I could use some help. I'm backed up on a lot of things, and having somebody around to help me out would be more than enough payback for me. I'll give you a salary, plus bonuses."

I frowned. "I don't really have any skills."

"Can you use a computer?" he asked.

"Yes. I used them in libraries, and I got some skills in high school."

"Can you run errands?"

"Of course." My foot was pretty much healed, but Jett still needed to continue to baby his knee until his meniscus was completely healed. "My driver's license is expired, but I can renew it if I'm in one place for a while."

"You have no job experience?" he questioned, sounding more curious than worried that I'd never worked a real job.

I took a deep breath. It was time for me to share a little bit about my past with him. "My mom was a pastry chef. She and my grandmother had a catering company. I didn't really pull a paycheck, but Mom gave me some money for every event I helped out with. Gran always handled the food because she was an amazing chef, and Mom handled all the desserts. My dad ran the business part of things, so it was mainly a family business. I helped my mother with events from the time I was in grade school until I left Ohio at the age of seventeen."

"You've been on the streets since you were seventeen?" he asked with a frown.

I nodded, hoping he wouldn't ask me about anything else.

"Then you worked," Jett concluded. "Obviously you were a good assistant or your mom and dad wouldn't have kept taking you to the events."

I smiled. "I loved it. Eventually, I helped Mom do her baking, and I learned to do decent pastries myself. The only thing I'd ever wanted to do was keep on working in the catering business with my family."

Jett was silent for a moment before he asked in a husky voice, "What happened, Ruby? You were out on the streets when you should have been getting ready for high school graduation."

Since I didn't cry, I refused to acknowledge the tears that were welling in my eyes. I blinked them back before I answered. "We were on our way to a big event when I was sixteen. The roads were icy, and my dad lost control of the van. My father, my mother, and my gran died instantly. I only suffered some cuts, bruises, and a concussion. I don't remember most of the crash or what happened right after."

My one and only visit to the hospital had been the worst day of my entire life.

"Jesus, Ruby," Jett rasped. "I'm so fucking sorry. No wonder you're so damn afraid of hospitals."

I tried to swallow the enormous lump in my throat.

I'm not going to cry. Not in the middle of a nice restaurant. And not anywhere else, either.

"You didn't have any other family to go to?"

I stared at my half-filled wine glass, unable to look at Jett as I told him, "Only…my uncle."

"You have an uncle, and you're on the streets?"

Yeah, it was going to be hard to answer Jett's question, but I needed to be as honest with him as possible. He was trying to help me, so I owed him that.

"He was…abusive." I looked up at Jett, my eyes pleading with him not to ask me anything else.

He nodded sharply, like he understood that I didn't want to talk about my uncle. "What happened to your inheritance? There must have been money coming from the business, and I'm sure your parents had some funds."

I shook my head. "My uncle was a silent controlling partner. He'd given my dad the funds for startup, so he took over half ownership. He sold it. And since he was my only relative, he was also my guardian once my parents and grandma were gone."

"A house? Life insurance? Savings?" he asked.

"We rented our home, and we didn't have a lot of money," I told him. "We were one of those families who just got by."

"So you didn't really ever have a chance to work because you left home while you were a minor," he observed.

"Not much else except the catering business," I confessed. "I picked berries where I could for money while I was on the road. I did just about any unskilled labor I could to survive."

"Why South Florida if you were a Midwestern girl?"

"When you're homeless, it's better to be someplace warm. I can cool down during the day in the library, but it's hard to survive frigid temperatures."

"What about shelters?"

"I used them sometimes, but there was usually somebody who needed it more than me. Mothers with kids, someone elderly who couldn't survive the elements. There just isn't enough space for every homeless person."

"Come with me to Seattle, Ruby. Trust me just enough to know I'm never going to send you out on the streets again," Jett commanded in a guttural tone.

I knew he could never understand that I really trusted *no one.* Being alone and homeless, I couldn't. I'd already made a huge mistake by trusting the wrong people, and I'd had a smaller lesson that I'd learned on my own during my adult life on the road.

But Dani had stuck her neck out and helped me, even when she really had no idea whether or not I was worth saving. And then Jett had done the impossible and gotten me out of a bad situation at considerable risk to himself. He'd even been injured trying to save my ass.

We locked eyes, and I asked, "Is that really what you want?"

He nodded. "Maybe I need you as much as you need me."

I highly doubted that Jett Lawson really needed *anyone.* He appeared to be pretty self-contained. But if I could help him, and keep myself off the streets, I was willing to try to be useful to him.

"Then, yes. I'll go. But I'd really like to find a job as soon as possible." I had to take a huge leap of faith because there was no other option if I ever wanted my life back.

He actually looked relieved when I'd given him the answer he appeared to want.

Chapter 5

Ruby

We were back at the condo later that night, both of us hanging out in the living room, when a very big question hit me. I asked Jett in a flat tone, "What happens when you fall in love? I don't think any woman is going to want her man living with another woman, even if it isn't a sexual relationship and I'm just an employee."

I stopped downloading free books to the e-reader Jett had gotten me, and looked at him sitting in a recliner across the room.

If Jett suddenly fell in love, what would happen to me?

Since he'd asked me to marry him, I assumed he didn't have somebody waiting for him in Seattle, but I'd discovered that assumptions weren't always correct.

My stomach knotted at the idea of Jett being involved with a woman, and I wasn't quite sure why. It wasn't my fear of being alone again because I'd already been there. I was thinking the tightness in my belly had more to do with the fact that I was attracted to Jett.

Being drawn to Jett wasn't comfortable for me, but I couldn't seem to stop myself from staring at his gorgeous body and his handsome face. For some unknown reason, I just wanted to be closer to him. Something pulled me toward him even when I should really be pushing him away.

He shrugged. "That's not going to happen."

"Why in the world not?"

"No woman is going to want *me*," he said matter-of-factly. "And honestly, I have no desire to date anyway."

I looked at him, confused. "Why?"

He was quiet for a moment before he said, "I was engaged once. It didn't end well."

Riveted, I watched his eyes grow dark as he added, "We came pretty damn close to getting married. Fortunately, we put off setting a definite date."

"What happened?"

"*My accident* happened. Marcus headed a team of guys who formed a private rescue organization. We went in when the government wouldn't and rescued victims who were kidnapped and imprisoned in foreign countries. Usually political prisoners. We'd been together for years, saved a lot of lives. But our helicopter crashed in the Middle East. A couple of us were pretty badly wounded. It's been a few years, and I'm still not fully recovered."

"So *you* broke it off because of your accident?" Why would he do that when he must have needed support?

"*She* broke it off. I didn't get the best of medical care because we weren't close to a large city right after the accident. By the time I got back to the States, they weren't sure they could save my leg, and I looked like hell. I still am, and always will be badly scarred. Lisette hated the way I looked, and she didn't want me with a bum leg that would keep me from doing a lot of things, especially dancing or any other social activity that required some kind of grace."

"She dumped you because you couldn't dance?" I asked incredulously.

"I'm pretty sure she didn't want a guy who was going to be scarred for the rest of his life, either."

"Oh, my God, are you kidding me?" My shocked question rang out louder than it should have, but I was pretty damn dumbfounded.

"You wanted honesty, Ruby. I'm spilling my guts here," he informed me drily.

"I'm sorry. I just can't imagine any woman in her right mind dumping you for such a superficial reason." Honestly, I was angry. Jett had been saving others when he'd been hurt. "What kind of bitch does something like that?"

His eyes lightened with humor, but he didn't speak. He shut down the laptop he was holding, and set it aside.

Finally, he said, "I guess the kind of woman I was going to marry would do something like that."

I put my e-reader on the side table as I asked, "Do you still love her?"

Please say no!

Jett didn't deserve to be pining over a woman who *definitely* hadn't loved *him*.

"I don't," he answered gruffly. "Hell, I don't even *like* her anymore. Haven't seen her since she walked out of my hospital room after reminding me what a mess I was. But that experience pretty much told me that very few women were ever going to be able to overlook the fact that I have...limitations. And some pretty ugly scars."

He thought he wasn't attractive anymore? Surely Jett didn't think that no other woman would want him just because he'd been dissed by a grade-A bitch. "That's not true," I said emphatically. "You're still very attractive."

"You haven't seen me naked," he rumbled.

It wasn't the first time he'd said that in some kind of joking form, but I wished he'd quit reminding me that I really *would* like to see his ripped body completely in the raw.

I wanted to tell him that I'd love to see him nude, but I wasn't brave enough to admit that I couldn't find a single fault in him. His scars were just a part of *him*, proof that he was willing to do anything—even risk his own life—to save someone else. If that wasn't a turn-on for some women, it was their loss.

I thought about what he had told me, and all I did was get more and more pissed off. "She's not the only type of woman out there, Jett. In fact, I'd say she was an exception."

"Not in my world," he snapped.

"Then maybe you need to find a new world," I suggested.

"I don't feel like looking for somebody else, Ruby," he replied. "I'd rather put my effort into my company, and making a full recovery. My knee will never be quite right, but I'm hoping it will get better than what it is now. The surgeries are over, I hope. I had my last one on my knee a few months ago. So it's all about working on getting it stronger."

I hadn't known Jett when his accident happened, but I wanted to be around for him now. Some woman had done a number on him, and he needed to stop looking at the world around him through a cynical pair of glasses. "I'll help you as much as I can," I vowed. "And it sounds like losing your fiancée was actually a gift. Maybe it doesn't feel that way right now, but someday it will."

"Maybe I was a little clueless back then, but I knew I'd made a lucky escape the minute she walked out the door," he said hoarsely.

"But she hurt you," I argued.

"Maybe. But it would have hurt more if I'd married her."

It was entirely possible that Jett was over his ex, but I was fairly certain that he'd never gotten over the rejection itself if he thought there weren't a million women out there who would snap him up immediately if they had the chance. Dancing skill or not.

Jett was special.

But he didn't seem to recognize that he was a whole lot more than just a few scars.

"I think you're gorgeous," I blurted out before I could stop the words from flying out of my mouth.

I didn't retract my statement. Scars included, Jett was one of the hottest guys I'd ever met. He was completely ripped, and I knew he'd been using the gym in the condo to keep up his exercise routine. I hadn't liked that at first, but he'd explained that he could lift weights without stressing his knee. And he'd start back again with his regular routine to strengthen his leg once he was sure the meniscus had healed.

He crossed his arms in front of him, his biceps flexing as he asked, "What in the hell is attractive about me now?"

I considered his skeptical expression and the way he had one of his brows raised in question.

I melted as I realized he really didn't see *a single good thing* about himself anymore.

"I love your eyes," I said honestly, not exactly wanting to tell him that I lusted after his body. "Did you know they change when you're happy and when you're angry? But every shade is beautiful. Your eyes are truly green and not hazel. Did you know that's the rarest eye color? Only two percent of people in the world have green eyes."

He was trying to resist the urge to smile, but he didn't completely accomplish it. "More reading at the library?" he asked with a smirk.

I shrugged. "I told you that strange facts or quotes I've read come out of my mouth at the weirdest of times. But what I say is factual. And yeah, it's information I picked up in the library."

"What else do you find attractive about me?" he asked hesitantly.

Okay. I was done holding back because I could see he wasn't quite believing what I said. "You're completely ripped, and every time I see your ass in a pair of jeans, I want to take a bite out of it."

"I'm scarred, woman. Are you fucking blind? You saw a small preview the night I got you out of the club."

I crossed my arms stubbornly. "When I admire your tight butt, I'm not exactly thinking about your *scars*."

"You're a virgin. What do you know about nice asses?"

"Maybe I haven't touched, but I can sure as hell look."

A bark of laughter escaped him before he answered, "I give up. You have no idea how *unattractive* a messed-up body looks naked. Do you always look for something good in everybody?"

"That's not hard to do with a guy like you," I said in a breathless voice. "Other than your scars and your bossiness, you're pretty much perfect. I think your ex was crazy to give you up."

"But *you* didn't want to marry me," he countered.

"I wanted to say yes," I confessed. "But you don't deserve to be stuck with a woman like me. I've been homeless all my adult life, Jett. I have no job skills, and I didn't have any kind of future. You've already put out more money to save me than I'm worth. *Way* more. And it wouldn't have been a marriage that was happening for the right reasons."

Jett would have done it because he wanted to rescue me, and even though I liked him, my primary reason for marriage would have been to have a roof over my head and some kind of stability.

"Nothing that happened to you was your fault, Ruby," Jett growled.

"My uncle didn't want me to leave. I left of my own free will," I said nervously.

Jett stood and walked slowly over to the couch to sit next to me. "Tell me what happened, Ruby. Just throw it out there. I'm not going to judge. If he was abusive, you *had* to leave."

"I didn't *have* to, but once the rest of my family was gone, I had no reason to take his abuse anymore. He was an alcoholic for as long as I can remember, and whenever he drank, he got violent. I-I couldn't take it anymore," I stammered.

"Son of a bitch!" Jett said harshly. "What happened after the accident? I'm sure your parents protected you from him before it happened."

"I lived with him for almost a year, just long enough to make sure I could leave without him finding me until after I'd turned eighteen. His violent temper escalated into insanity. I had to leave with almost nothing to my name. Their part of the business would end up being his, and I couldn't stay there."

Jett pulled my trembling body against his, and I let his strong body support mine as I leaned into him. I mumbled against his shoulder, "I just couldn't do it anymore. I wanted to graduate from high school, but there were times I didn't think I'd live that long. I had to go."

Jett stroked his hand down my back in a comforting way that made me feel safe as he replied, "You shouldn't have ever been abused in the first place."

He sounded disgusted. Not that I blamed him. Abuse was not only painful, but it was humiliating, too. And I'd felt every moment of my shame. I still did.

I continued so I could get everything out without crying. "Looking back now, I know I should have gone to somebody at school or something after my parents died. But I was scared, and I didn't know what would happen to me. I just wanted to be old enough to get out."

His arm tightened around my waist as he answered gutturally, "I'll protect you, Ruby. You don't have to be afraid anymore."

I melted into him. Usually, I didn't like *anybody* touching me, but with Jett, for some reason, I felt…safe.

Chapter 6

Jett

L ater that night, I lay in bed listening to the sound of the waves hitting the shore on the beach, but it didn't have the calming effect it usually did for me.

I was fucking irritated, wrestling with emotions I'd never experienced before, and I hated it.

I'd told myself that I wanted Ruby to trust me like the brother she'd never had after she'd refused to marry me, but that was a difficult thing to wish for when I didn't *really* feel that way.

Truth was, I wanted to be her protector.

I wanted to be the person she turned to when she needed something or if she wanted to confide in somebody.

But I totally *didn't want* to be like a brother to her.

Ruby Kent had grabbed me by the balls the very same night I'd met her, and she hadn't let go since the evening she'd accidentally put both of us in the hospital.

My marriage proposal had been instinctive, a response to the vow I'd made to myself right after Lisette had dumped me in the hospital. The moment I realized that Ruby didn't really react to my scars, and I knew she had a heart, I'd blurted out the promise I'd made to myself after the accident.

I'd asked her to marry me.

And she'd said *no*.

When I'd discovered that she was refusing because she didn't think I deserved to be stuck with *her*, it had made me even more determined to make her mine.

Protective, possessive instincts had slammed me in the gut, and they'd stayed there, strengthening with every damn moment I spent in Ruby's company. I hated the fact that nobody had been there for her when she was getting beat up. In fact, it made me pretty crazy to think about anybody touching her. *Period.*

I grinned as I stared up at the high ceiling. She could be a handful sometimes, but I kind of liked that about her. She was intelligent and inquisitive, and she'd needed the heart of a lion to get through all of the challenges she'd faced. And she was definitely prone to voicing her opinions, especially when she was angry. She'd been quiet at first, almost pensive right after she'd thrown my proposal back in my face. But as time went on, she was speaking up more often and more vehemently.

Except for my sisters, no female had ever leapt to my defense like Ruby did. My ex-fiancée had been a selfish woman, and I'd somehow just let myself fall into a routine of trying to make her happy. Unfortunately, I never *really* did pull that off. The more I'd given to Lisette, the more she'd wanted. When I'd had the audacity to change my appearance by getting badly injured, she thought *she* was the one who had the right to be angry because I'd screwed up her vision of a perfect future.

I hadn't been lying to Ruby when I'd said that I *knew* I'd made a lucky escape.

The deadness I felt inside me had nothing to do with the fact that I didn't marry a woman who had never loved me. But Lisette had left me a legacy of doubt, and a whole lot of wondering whether she was right about me never finding somebody who would overlook my flaws.

After the accident, my priorities changed. *I* had changed.

I'd realized that life would never be without challenges for any couple, and I preferred to be alone if I didn't have someone who cared enough about me to be there during the difficult times.

And I wanted somebody who would want *me* there with them, too.

Unlike my two older brothers, I'd never really been a player. I'd never had any desire to go through a bunch of different women in a short period of time.

All I'd wanted was a woman who loved me.

I didn't have a reluctance to trust or commit like Carter and Mason seemed to possess, either.

Unfortunately, I'd chosen the wrong woman to settle down with, and I was relieved that I hadn't married her.

Everything had been okay with Lisette when things were easy, and we were a golden couple with no problems before my accident. I guessed that the real test for Lisette and me was when shit hit the fan, because she had bolted when things got ugly, and not without a scathing lecture about how I'd messed up her perfect life.

Luckily, I'd had plenty of family. Maybe we'd drifted apart, but my siblings had been there when I was in the hospital.

My self-worth suffered sometimes, but I'd never been completely by myself to deal with every challenge I'd faced.

Not like Ruby.

Although her scars were on the inside, I knew that she was damaged in a way I'd never understand because I'd never walked in her shoes. Maybe the fact that she still seemed amazed by small things, and the way she seemed to live in the moment instead of dwelling on her past surprised me.

Hell, I wanted to give her *everything* just so I could see her reaction every single time she got something new. But I knew she'd draw the line on expensive stuff.

I should have told her that I have more money than a person could spend in a lifetime of complete gluttony.

But it felt pretty good that she liked me as a regular guy and not a billionaire.

Ruby was smart, and I was surprised that she hadn't yet connected the Lawson name to Lawson Technologies.

But then, I'd never really hinted at the fact that my company was anything other than a small business.

Honestly, I hadn't cared much about anything except getting her to go home to Seattle with me, because there was no damn way I was leaving her here in Miami. Yeah, maybe I'd offered to set her up here, but that wasn't what I wanted, and if she'd chosen that option, I would have found a way to change her mind. Either that, or I would be spending a lot of time down south.

My main objective was to make sure she was never hurt again.

Ruby belonged with *me,* and I wanted her to be somewhere that I could watch out for her, even if it killed me.

"It's *definitely* going to kill me," I mumbled at the ceiling.

Every day I spent with her was another day that I wanted nothing more than to make her mine.

I craved her with an intensity that made my gut ache, but she'd been abused, and she'd had nobody she could trust in the world. I was determined to be *the* guy who Ruby could believe in, regardless of the fact that I couldn't be around her without getting blue balls.

I can't fuck her.

It was good enough for now that she didn't cringe at my scars in the car that first night.

I *could* make Ruby my friend.

But I wasn't about to make her my lover, no matter what my dick was demanding. It would make things way too complicated for her. I was going to have to be patient.

More than anything, Ruby needed to trust me. And after what had happened with her uncle, I didn't want to scare her away.

She fucking deserves so much better than what life has given her so far.

Ruby needed to be safe, and she needed some sense of security.

If nothing else, I could give her both of those things and a hell of a lot more.

In return, I'd have a woman who didn't treat me like an invalid.

For now, that was going to have to be enough.

Chapter 7

Ruby

I woke up gasping for breath, and trying to free myself from the strong arms that were confining me.

"Let go of me!" I screamed.

I was instantly freed, leaving me confused and terrified.

"Ruby, you were dreaming. You were screaming."

Jett?

I recognized his comforting baritone almost immediately.

I wrapped my arms around myself protectively, my conscious mind beginning to slowly work again.

I'd been in the grips of a nightmare, one of many that I'd experienced in my life.

Taking slower breaths, I began to calm down, and my eyes opened to the dim light.

I'm with Jett. I'm safe.

I turned my head and saw Jett sitting patiently on the other side of the massive king-sized bed. He'd obviously moved away from me when he realized I needed space.

I ran a shaky hand through my hair. "Oh, God. I'm so sorry. I have nightmares sometimes."

It was the first one I'd had since I'd been staying with Jett. Had I thought about it when I'd come to the condo, I would have taken the bedroom farthest away from his. I never got much of a reprieve from my nightmares.

"Don't be sorry, sweetheart," Jett answered in a low, husky baritone. "You can't exactly control them."

His slow, easy tone calmed me down.

I'm with Jett. I'm safe.

Those words were becoming my mantra, and it was comforting to know I wasn't alone. "But I didn't mean to wake you up. Was I loud?"

"Loud enough to scare the shit out of me," he answered in a troubled voice.

The only light in the room was coming from the hallway, so I couldn't see his face. But I could tell that he was only wearing a pair of pajama bottoms. He hadn't bothered to cover his upper body before he'd come to see if I was okay.

"I didn't mean to yell at you," I said hesitantly. "Sometimes it takes me a few minutes to realize that I was dreaming. And I don't usually like anyone touching me in any way. Well, except for you sometimes."

I was still shivering, even though it wasn't cold. My pajamas had a T-shirt top and short bottoms, but I was covered in the sheet and blanket. My inability to stop trembling was simply the aftermath of the frightening dream.

"I get it," Jett said reassuringly. "I still have bad dreams about the accident occasionally. I don't remember a whole lot, but my memory must have retained some of it because those dreams are pretty damn vivid."

How was it that Jett always knew just what to say to make me feel like I'm not alone?

"Do you remember crashing?" I asked curiously.

"Only from my dreams. I'm not sure if it's what *really* occurred, or if it's only a nightmare not based on fact."

"Mine are real," I confessed softly. "And they're usually so scary that I can't get back to sleep."

"Are you okay now?" he questioned.

"I think so. Everything seems a lot easier since I met you."

I hadn't meant to blurt those words out, but they were true.

"Do you want me to stay with you?" he offered.

I wanted desperately to keep Jett here with me. "Only if you'll be comfortable."

He responded by getting up and opening the window, then made his way back to the bed and climbed underneath the covers, making himself comfortable for a moment before he was completely still.

I snuggled back down in the bed with a tired yawn.

Glancing at the clock, I noticed it was three o'clock in the morning, so it was no wonder that I still felt exhausted.

"You know you're wasting energy, right?" I asked Jett. "If you open the window, the air conditioning has to work harder."

"Just listen," he requested huskily.

I was silent, and it only took me a moment to recognize the sounds of the ocean. I sighed as the rhythmic noise of the waves hitting the shore lulled me into a more relaxed state.

Finally, Jett's voice broke the silence. "The sound of the ocean helps me remember that there are some things so much bigger and more powerful in life than my problems."

"It's amazing," I answered.

"Worth a little extra energy?" he asked with humor in his deep baritone.

I smiled. "Sometimes keeping your sanity is probably worth any price."

Honestly, I'd never had the luxury of experiencing the sense of calm I had right now. My life had always been about survival. There was no room for anything else except living through another day.

"I feel like Cinderella right now," I admitted. "None of this would be happening if it wasn't for you. And I'm still not quite sure how to deal with it."

"You don't have to do anything to handle it, *Cinderella*. Just let it be. You *should* have a home, and you *should* be able to feel safe. This country is supposed to be considered the land of opportunity, but sometimes circumstances screw you."

"Before my parents died, I wanted so many things. I dreamed about having my own catering business, and I'd fantasize about the day I could actually be…free."

My hopes for the future were the only thing that had gotten me through the bad times before I'd become an adult.

"Were you happy as a kid, Ruby?" he asked. "When your parents were alive, did you have a good life?"

I hesitated for a moment, but I finally answered, "I was happy with my mom and dad. We didn't have a lot of money, but my dad could always find a way to make things fun. And I knew that they loved me."

"All those things you wanted should have happened for you, Ruby," Jett said gruffly. "You got fucked over by life."

"I'm scared," I murmured, less afraid of expressing my fears to Jett in the darkness. "I don't understand why you're helping me, and I'm afraid it will all come to an end."

"You don't trust me yet," Jett said flatly. "But trust takes time, especially after all the things that happened to you."

"I'm a stranger to you, Jett."

"Not anymore," he grumbled. "And you'll eventually learn that I'm not going anywhere."

"Do you trust *me*?" I asked hesitantly.

"Yes," he said immediately.

"Why?"

"Because you haven't given me any reason *not* to trust you."

In truth, Jett had never given me any reason not to trust *him*, either. "I'm sorry. I should have more faith in people, I guess."

"Bullshit. You've never had a reason to trust anybody since your parents died. Our life experiences are different, Ruby. Other than my accident, I've led a pretty charmed life. You've never had that experience."

I let his words sink in. Our perspectives *were* incredibly different. "So you trust everybody until they give you a reason not to?"

He chuckled. "Hell, no. I'm a businessman. If I trusted everybody, they'd screw me over. But sometimes you know in your gut who to trust and who *not* to trust. I went with gut instinct with you, Cinderella."

"I'm not always a good person, Jett," I confessed. "Sometimes I was actually so hungry that I stole food. But I never stole money or other things. But when you're hungry—"

"Don't, Ruby," he warned in a dangerous tone. "Don't justify trying to survive."

"I'm not," I answered. "I guess I just want you to know everything bad about me. Since you trust me, you *deserve* to know."

"You never have to explain yourself to me."

"Maybe I *want* to talk about it."

"Then go ahead," he said unhappily.

I took a deep breath before I said, "When I was really hungry, I considered selling my body for money or food."

"Why didn't you?" he asked roughly.

"Because I decided I'd rather die than to let somebody use my body. I couldn't stand to just lay there and let somebody touch me just to get off. And what if they ended up violent like my uncle?"

I heard Jett's sharp intake of breath before he replied, "I want to hunt your uncle down and make him regret every fucking time he touched you."

His comment probably should have scared me, but instead, his protectiveness made my heart ache. Nobody had ever stood up for me. Nobody had ever tried to keep me safe. However, the last thing I wanted was for Jett to get himself in trouble. "He's not worth it," I said.

Jett released a masculine sigh. "Maybe not. But I think he needs to be investigated so this doesn't happen to another kid."

I'd actually never thought about that, and my stomach did a flip at the thought. "Maybe I should have talked. I never even considered that he might do that to another child."

"Of course you didn't," Jett replied in a softer tone. "You weren't in a position to be strong. He kept you controlled and underneath his thumb."

"Is there some way we can check him out to make sure he isn't doing this to anybody else?" I asked.

Jett chuckled. "Cinderella, you have no idea how much I'm capable of doing. I'm an expert hacker, and I have a lot of connections."

"You're a hacker?" I said, astonished.

"Not exactly. But cybersecurity is my specialty, so it goes with the job."

"Will you teach me?" I asked hopefully.

"Only if you promise not to try it on your own," he said thoughtfully. "It's pretty damn easy to get yourself in trouble if you don't know all the subtleties of getting in and out without a footprint."

"I promise," I said eagerly.

"What about your dreams of having your own catering company? You can't give that up to become a hacker. I do it because I'm testing the strength of systems. Otherwise, it's a crime."

I sighed. "I only wanted to learn because I pretty much want to know everything. And I'm never going to have a popular catering business. I think that's pretty much just a fantasy. There are a lot of startup costs, and I'd need to learn how to handle the business part of things. I'd hoped that I could manage to get some kind of business degree before my parents died."

"Don't ever let go of your dreams, Ruby," he warned.

"There are *dreams,* and then there's *reality.* My real life was way too far away from my dreams to even consider starting my own business after my parents died. I just wanted to get a job. Any job. But when you're dirty, homeless, and have absolutely no skills, nobody is going to take a chance on somebody like that."

"I'm willing," he shot back.

"Yeah," I agreed. "Sometimes I have to wonder if your brain is completely functional."

"I have an IQ of 155, so I'm technically a genius," he said with mock defensiveness. "And I double majored in business and cybersecurity in college, but I was already a damn good hacker even before I went to school."

"Okay, so maybe there's just one tiny portion of your brain that's dysfunctional," I answered as I smiled.

I'd already known that Jett was gifted. He carried around a lot more useless facts in his head than I did.

"Not true," he insisted. "I guess you just need to understand that you deserve every dream you've ever imagined."

His words made me mute. I'd never believed that I was worth much of anything. I'd never felt worthy of being pulled out of homelessness and poverty. Probably because my self-esteem had always been bad.

"Thank you," I finally said in a quiet but sincere tone.

"For what?"

"For being you," I replied simply.

What else could I say? There was no way to really explain how special Jett was.

"I'm not all that great," he muttered humbly.

Fun fact: Jett knew how to encourage and look after other people, but he didn't think it was a big deal or that he was special in any way.

"You *are* pretty great," I answered sleepily. "You just don't see it."

I closed my eyes, and fell back to sleep to the sounds of the ocean.

Maybe it was the knowledge that Jett was so close that kept any and all bad dreams away for the rest of the night.

Chapter 8

Ruby

"You know what happened to you wasn't normal, right?"
I fidgeted on the couch I had planted my ass on when
I'd entered the psychologist's office.

Dr. Annette Romain was a pleasant and insightful therapist as far
as I could tell. But she asked probing questions that weren't all that
easy to talk about. Somehow, she'd seemed to wring things from
my soul that had been so deeply buried that I thought they would
never rise to the surface.

But as all of my emotions reemerged, so did my sense of hopelessness and sorrow.

I'd already spilled everything about my uncle, things that I'd never
told *anyone*, not even Jett.

After Jett had discovered my history, or what he knew about it,
he'd booked an appointment with a counselor for me today. Logically,
I knew I had issues from my past, but I didn't necessarily *want* to face
them or have them brought out. I would have preferred to just forget.

I looked up at the blonde woman sitting in a chair across from my
position on the couch.

Did I know that my life hadn't been normal? "It was all I knew," I finally answered honestly.

She nodded. "When it's the *only* life you've known, it's easy to start thinking it's normal, or at least it's *your* normal, even when you know the majority of young people your age have an entirely different reality."

"Sometimes I feel like I did something to deserve it," I confessed quietly.

"You didn't," Dr. Romain said firmly. "You were a child. The issues were your uncle's and *never* yours. You were an innocent victim who developed coping skills that you aren't going to need anymore."

"Like my trust issues?" I asked. "I don't trust anyone. I'm not sure I ever can."

"A certain amount of caution is a good thing, but not trusting somebody who has never given you reason not to have faith in them can be detrimental, Ruby."

"I'm afraid to trust Jett," I blurted out. "Even after all he's done to help me, I'm just waiting for the next bad thing to happen to me. I'm waiting for the bomb to drop on this whole Cinderella fantasy I'm living right now. Maybe that's not fair, but I can't control those fears."

"Ruby, you need to be patient and give yourself some time. You're anxious, and that's common for anybody who has gone through the kind of trauma that you've experienced. But I want to help you sort out what's reasonable fear, and what isn't. And I want you to really understand that none of your past was ever your fault. Nor was your homelessness."

Unshed tears were blurring my vision and I blinked them away as I said, "I'd like that. I don't want to live my whole life being afraid."

"You're brave, Ruby. I know you don't see that right now, but I hope that you *will* eventually. You survived five years on the streets with no resources except your intelligence. The fact that you came out of that relatively unscathed is pretty extraordinary. You used the resources available to you as best you could to get through having no stable place to live."

I sighed. "I don't feel *smart*. I feel like a *loser*."

"Is it logical for you to feel that way? You had no other choices."

"I guess I'm finding out that my feelings and logic don't really jive together all that well."

Dr. Romain sent me an empathetic smile. "Many times, they don't. Especially when you come from a highly dysfunctional and abusive background. Your reality is different."

My *reality* had always been all about survival. "I don't know anything else except how to stay alive anymore," I admitted hesitantly.

"Of course you don't," Dr. Romain said gently. "But now that you're safe, those instincts that served you well before will hamper you as you try to build a life for yourself."

I knew she was right. If I was always fearful about when the next bomb was going to drop, it was going to be hard to concentrate on anything else. Jett had given me opportunity, and a home. I didn't want to blow my chance at a new life because of old baggage.

"I don't want to be afraid anymore," I told her as the tears continued to threaten. "And I want to be able to trust Jett. He's helped me so much, and I don't think he has a single ulterior motive in giving me a hand up. But that's hard for me to accept. Who does that? Who helps someone they don't even know?"

"Ruby, some people *do that*. Good people. Plenty of them do exist. For what it's worth, Mr. Lawson *is* worried about you. I talked to him at length when he contacted me to make an appointment for you. He grilled me about everything from my methods of counseling to my education."

"He talked to you about me?" I asked with surprise.

"Just the basics of your situation, and I won't be speaking to him again. Now that I've seen you as a patient, anything you tell me will always be confidential. But he wanted to make sure I was the right counselor for you."

"See, I don't understand that. Why does he care about me? I'm nobody to him."

Dr. Romain held out a box of tissues. I took them, but didn't remove any from the box. I wasn't crying, and I didn't plan on crying. But my voice was cracking with emotion.

"Some people do care, Ruby. You just haven't experienced that side of humanity very much. But it does exist. Your parents sound like they were very good people, but they didn't have anything to give. They were focused on you and the survival of your family. Does the fact that Jett cares scare you?"

"Yes. But I'm grateful that he does."

"You deserve it, and you should have had somebody who cared that you were homeless long before now," Dr. Romain said firmly. "We just need to get you to the point where you know that you're worthy of taking a hand up."

"Then you have a lot of work to do," I mumbled.

"Are you afraid of Jett?" she probed.

I shook my head. "No. I'm not afraid *of* him. I'm just scared that I'll disappoint him."

"So you like him?" she asked. "Sometimes it's hard to get close to a man after you've been abused by one."

"He'd never abuse me," I said emphatically. "I can't say I completely understand what he's doing, but I know he wants to help me. I just don't understand why."

"Then he's probably the first person you could learn to trust," Dr. Romain told me.

"I'm attracted to him," I blurted out, telling my counselor the one thing that was really eating at me. "I know it's weird because I hardly know him, but I've been drawn to him from the beginning. And I've actually never felt this way before."

"Sexually attracted?" she asked to clarify.

I nodded. "Yes. But it's more than just that. I feel like we understand each other even though we come from completely different worlds. He's been hurt, both physically and emotionally. I guess that's why I connect with him. We've both known pain, but in different ways."

Dr. Romain sighed. "I have to caution you about getting involved with anybody on a sexual level. Until you can trust, I don't think it's a good idea. You need time to heal, Ruby. But you can deepen your friendship and learn to be okay with him helping you."

I rolled my eyes. "Like he'd ever want me anyway? I find it highly unlikely. But feeling attracted to him isn't comfortable for me."

"Why wouldn't he want you, Ruby?" she asked softly.

"Because I'm a nobody, and he's a successful guy. Why would he want a homeless woman who never even finished high school?"

"You can get your GED very easily," she argued gently. "And then continue on with college if that's what you want. You're very well spoken, and intelligent."

"Too much time cooling off in the library," I said flatly. "I spent many of my days in the library, and I read a lot. I always have, even as a kid."

"That's good," she said. "I'm going to send you home with a workbook that has exercises for you to do between our sessions."

"I'll do them," I said in a rush. I'd do almost anything to get over my anxiety and fears.

She nodded. "Are you ready to talk about your uncle and life growing up?"

I wanted to because it would probably help to get my past out in the open between us, but I finally shook my head. "Not yet. Not him."

It'd been hard enough for me to cough up the basic information. I wasn't ready to go in-depth about every occurrence.

"That's perfectly okay," she replied. "We don't have to discuss it to get you going on cognitive therapy. But I hope you'll be comfortable enough eventually, and if you want, to file charges in Ohio."

Honestly, I wasn't sure I'd ever be okay with talking about my uncle, but ever since Jett had mentioned the fact that this could happen to somebody else, I knew I was going to have to talk. There had already been too much time for him to find another victim.

"I just can't talk about *him* right now," I admitted. I got nauseous every time I even *thought* about my uncle.

"Then maybe you can tell me why, after all we've discussed, you refuse to cry?"

Oh, no. I *really* didn't want to go there. "Because my uncle loved to make me cry," I answered simply.

She nodded. "Tell me more about your relationship with your parents?" Dr. Romain suggested, changing the subject. "Did you love them?"

I nodded. "Yes. I loved my grandmother, too. When they died, I had nobody."

"Yet you managed to survive. You should be proud of that instead of being ashamed. Most people will never know that kind of hardship, Ruby."

I thought for a moment and let everything she'd just said really sink into my brain.

I could at least consider the possibility that nothing that happened was *my* fault. But it was hard to let go of a lifetime of blaming myself for everything.

"Jett is giving me a chance to make my own future," I said, thinking aloud. "It's my turn to choose."

"Take the help he's giving. You're entitled to a chance to make your own life now," she suggested.

"I've always felt guilty," I said softly. "I'm not sure I can get away from that."

"We're going to work on changing those feelings, Ruby," Dr. Romain said reassuringly.

"I'm ready," I told her.

Judging by this first session, counseling was going to be agonizingly painful, but I hoped with Dr. Romain's help, I'd come out of it feeling a lot more confident and ready to take on the world from a way different position than I'd been in before I'd met Jett.

I didn't ever want to feel helpless and hopeless again.

Chapter 9

Ruby

"Did you know that Seattle was the home of the first gas station in the world when it was built in 1907?" I asked Jett as I got ready to put a pan of lasagna in the oven. He'd mentioned that the Italian dish was one of his favorites, and had asked if we could hit a restaurant that served it. I'd insisted on getting the groceries and making it myself now that my foot was completely healed. If nothing else, I could at least feed Jett since I had the skills.

I'd been through four sessions of counseling with Dr. Romain, and I'd been doing my homework every single night. I couldn't say I'd seen *a ton* of improvement, but I was slowly losing my fear of something bad happening. Slowly, I was just allowing myself to enjoy the time I spent with Jett without questioning it.

He looked up from the laptop he was using at the kitchen table. "Exactly how many facts do you have in that head of yours?" he joked.

"About seventeen years of them," I answered. "I started going to our local library in Ohio when I was five, and I never stopped."

"I live in Seattle, but I had no idea the first gas station was built there," he answered.

"But you didn't grow up there, right?" I asked curiously as I turned my back to him while I put the final layer of cheese on top of the mountain of meat, pasta, and cheese I'd prepared.

"I grew up in Rocky Springs, Colorado," he verified.

"What's it like in Colorado?"

He chuckled. "Rocky Springs is quiet. Pretty much a night and day difference between Seattle and Rocky Springs."

"Why did you leave?" I asked curiously.

"When my parents died, I guess all of us wanted to get away, and my company was getting too big to stay away from a big tech city."

"But Harper and Dani are there now," I mentioned.

"Both of them were wanderers. Harper is an architect, and she moved around building homeless shelters. And Dani was a foreign correspondent who was covering mostly the Middle East. So they never really made a home for themselves anywhere else."

"So you knew the Colter family from childhood?"

I was aware of the Colter family, even though I didn't exactly follow the news of the super-rich. I recognized the Colter name because Blake Colter was a senator, and he was vocal about his opinions.

"Yep," he affirmed. "I was friends with all of them, and my parents were friends with their mom. But I mostly stayed in contact with Marcus, and then we were even tighter once he formed PRO."

I put the lasagna in the oven and grabbed a couple of sodas from the fridge, setting one in front of Jett before I sat in the chair across the table from him. "Do you ever regret it because of your accident?" I asked. "Do you wish you'd never gotten involved in PRO?"

"Never," he said as he closed his laptop. "We saved a lot of lives, many of them women and kids. If I had the choice, I'd do it all over again. I lived through the accident, and they would have died if Marcus hadn't formed PRO."

"Wouldn't somebody else just have taken your place?" I popped the top on my soda and took a sip.

He shrugged. "Maybe. But they wouldn't have been as good as I am, and they may not have been successful at locating those women and kids. Marcus asked my brother Carter to sign up, too, but it wasn't his thing. I did fine solo."

I thought it was interesting how Jett brushed off most compliments, but he was pretty damn cocky when it came to his technical skills. He always claimed to be the world's best hacker.

Since he was gifted, he was probably right.

I leaned back in the chair and crossed my arms. "So you're the best? There's *nobody* better than you are?"

Jett and I had recently fallen into a pattern of challenging each other, and joking around about little things.

He shot me a mischievous grin. "Without a doubt. I've never met a system that I couldn't breech. Which is why I'm so good at designing systems to protect from a cyberattack."

I felt his brash smile way down to my toes, and everywhere in between. My heart skittered, and I tried to ignore the flutter in my stomach as I looked at him.

Jett was still an enigma to me. He was unlike any guy I'd ever met.

"When are you going to start teaching me about what you do? I'd like to get familiar with your company if I'm going to help you."

"We'll wait until we get back to Seattle," he said.

"I started researching some basic programming on the computer. Maybe if I can learn some of the basics, it will help." Computers weren't exactly one of my strong areas since I'd had very little time to work on them as an adult. But I already knew the basics, and I could learn.

"Ruby, I want you to do whatever you want to do. Once you get a GED, you'll be able to go to college if that's what you want, and that should come first," he grumbled as he popped the top on his soda and took a gulp.

"I can handle both," I argued. "And paying you back for what you did for me comes first."

"I don't give a damn about the money," he rumbled as he met my gaze.

"It matters to me, Jett," I answered honestly. "I need to feel good about myself, and that won't happen unless I do something to pay you back."

"Can't you ever just let somebody do something for you and just say thank you?" he asked gruffly. "I'm not keeping track, Ruby. And I wouldn't take it even if you *tried* to pay me back."

"Then I just won't draw a paycheck, and I'll eventually work enough to pay you," I answered stubbornly.

"You're cleaning, doing laundry, and cooking me meals. I hope you're deducting all of those hours as work," he snapped, sounding slightly injured.

"That's nothing. It's something I'd be doing if we were roommates or if I had my own place."

"Add it to your hours worked," he demanded in an irritated tone. "You're going to need those hours because I suppose you're going to throw *this* in my face, too."

He reached into his pocket and tossed me a small book the size of my hand.

I picked it up, recognizing the object immediately.

"I found it on the kitchen counter," he explained. "Since it's a national bank, all I had to do was drop in and make a deposit."

I turned the worn paper book around in my hand. Even though I was pretty sure the bank no longer issued the books, I'd had it since I was a kid. "It's my savings account book, but there was nothing left in it." I'd drawn every penny I could from the account when I'd left Ohio. It had only been a couple hundred dollars, but it had helped in the very beginning to buy food and a few other things I'd needed.

"There's money in there now," he muttered.

I opened it, but I didn't see a recent deposit, which made me more certain that the books were obsolete. All he'd probably needed was the account number.

I looked at him, astonished. "Why?"

He stood up, but his emerald gaze was still pinning me to my chair with its intensity. "Because if something should happen to me, I have to know that you'll be okay. Your days on the streets are done, Ruby. If I get hit by a truck tomorrow, you'll still be okay."

I wanted to tell him that I *wouldn't* be okay if something happened to him. I'd be devastated. Because *he* was more important than *his money.*

"I'm not your responsibility, Jett. I'm a grown woman." My reply came out harsh because I was still not good with thinking about his demise.

"I'm *making* you my responsibility because I *want* to," he answered in a graveled tone. "And I need to know you're going to be okay even if I'm not around."

"Why?" I asked hesitantly, not even wanting to consider any day that didn't have Jett in it.

"Because I fucking care about you, Ruby. Don't you get that?"

I shook my head. "I don't think that I *do* understand."

What Dr. Romain had said during our first day of counseling drifted through my mind.

My uncle hadn't protected me. He'd hurt me. And we were related.

But Jett, somebody who had only met me several weeks ago, was concerned about my future?

I wasn't sure how to reconcile that.

But I finally answered, "Please understand that *nobody* has ever cared about me since my parents died, Jett. *Nobody* has ever tried to protect me over the years that I've been homeless. *Nobody* really cared."

"I fucking care," he answered in a clipped baritone. "You can accept that or not. You don't have to spend the money if you don't want to. But keep it because it means something to me. It gives me peace of mind."

I looked at his tense expression, the muscle in his strong jaw twitching with irritation right before his face went completely blank. He started to walk away from the table, probably headed for the office where the computer equipment was set up.

I'd hurt him.

I knew it.

And that was the last thing I wanted to do to Jett.

My heart was aching as I cried out, "Wait. Please don't run away."

I jumped up from my chair and moved in front of him. My pride and confusion wasn't nearly as important as what he'd done for me.

My vision was blurred as I looked up at him, but I refused to cry. "I admit that I'm not sure how to deal with somebody who cares, but what you did—nobody has ever done something like that for me except my parents who opened that account for me a few decades ago. Thank you."

"Is that the end of your protest, Cinderella?" he asked as he raised my chin gently with his fingertips.

"I won't spend the money unless I need to," I warned him.

He nodded curtly. "I can live with that."

"But please know that it means a lot to me," I requested as I took his hand from my face and held it tightly.

He twined our fingers together. "I also did it so you'd feel safer. I guess I wanted you to know that you're always going to be okay. Nobody can take that security away from you, Ruby."

My heart was racing as I felt his warm breath on my face. I wanted to sink into Jett and stay there, absorbing his strength.

One of his motives in depositing money in my account had been just for me. So I'd realize that even if something happened, and he wanted to get rid of me, I'd always have funds.

Yes, getting dumped back on the streets was a really big fear for me, but I was getting more and more comfortable with the fact that Jett was never going to do that. "You didn't have to do that," I said in a whisper, my voice failing me as I looked into the eyes of the kindest man I'd ever known.

"I *wanted* to," he corrected hoarsely.

His whiskey-smooth baritone skittered down my spine and landed directly between my thighs. In that moment, I wanted nothing more than to have Jett kiss me.

His lips were inches from mine, and I was mesmerized by being so close to him. We stood like that for a moment. When I realized he wasn't going to make a move, I made one of my own.

I wrapped my hand around the back of his neck and pulled him down to meet me as I rose up on my toes.

Our lips met awkwardly, but Jett immediately took control. Pulling our fingers apart, he wrapped both arms around my waist, bringing me closer while he ravaged my mouth.

I moaned against his lips as I put my arms around his neck, needing to press my body against his to become submerged in his heat.

I was disappointed when he finally pulled his mouth from mine, but when he started to explore the sensitive skin of my neck, I let out an animalistic sound of need that I'd never heard come from my lips before.

"God, Ruby, I want you so damn much," he said huskily, his breath wafting over my ear, and making me ache for so much more.

"I need to touch you," I pleaded, tugging at the hem of his T-shirt.

All I wanted was to explore his bare flesh, and I yanked until he finally pulled the T-shirt over his head and dropped it on the floor.

My hands were all over him, running over every gorgeous muscle of his torso, getting drunk off the feel of his hard body before he pulled me against him again.

His hands stroked down my back until they landed on my jean-clad rear and squeezed.

I froze, my mind suddenly flooded with memories I'd just wanted to forget.

"Don't," I said in panic. "I can't do this. I can't look at the scars—" I broke off to twist my body away from his, desperate to get out of his hold.

He let me go the moment he realized that something was wrong.

We were both panting as we stared at each other.

"I'm sorry," I said breathlessly right before I sprinted toward my bedroom so I could be alone to try to clear my head.

But I was afraid that I couldn't outrun my thoughts, and no amount of time alone would ever get them out of my mind.

Chapter 10

Ruby

"We can leave for Seattle tomorrow," Jett informed me in a polite but distant tone a few days after my meltdown.

After what happened, I had managed to get my head together, but my relationship with Jett had irrevocably changed, and I was still mourning the gruff but sweet Jett who had been present *before* I'd flipped out on him.

We'd just finished dinner, and I set a dessert plate in front of him that contained a pretty simple pastry I'd made earlier in the afternoon.

"I thought we were waiting to make sure we didn't need to give more statements."

He shook his head, but he didn't look at me. "Your kidnappers took a deal. They agreed to plead guilty to lesser charges. They're testifying against one of the bigger fish above them in the food chain."

I sat down across from him since my rubbery legs didn't seem to want to hold me up. "Then it's...over?"

"It's over," he verified. "The two of them aren't getting out of jail time, but with lesser charges they might eventually see the light of day before they die."

"Thank God," I said in a shaky voice as I pushed my dark hair away from my face. "I didn't want to have to testify. Honestly, I didn't even want to give another statement."

"You got your wish," he said flatly. "Can you be ready to leave tomorrow morning?"

"Yes," I answered, grateful that I'd be able to start my life somewhere else.

Since I really, really didn't want to have to go through my whole history with another counselor, Dr. Romain, who I now called Annette by her request, had agreed to doing video sessions when I moved with Jett to Seattle, so I wouldn't really miss any of my counseling.

"Are you sure you still want me?" I asked hesitantly.

"Of course I'm sure," he answered brusquely.

"I know you're angry—"

"I'm not mad at *you*, Ruby. I'm pretty much pissed off at myself. It never should have happened," he said firmly.

"I *wanted* it to happen," I told him quietly.

Annette and I had already discussed my involuntary reaction, and she'd told me it was normal. But it didn't feel natural to me to reject Jett in any way. Not anymore.

He finally looked up and pinned me with his turbulent gaze. "No, you didn't want it to happen. I think you feel like you *owe* me something, and maybe you didn't want me to feel rejected. But the last thing I want from you is a pity fuck."

I was shocked into silence. *Is that what he thought? That I was willing to screw him to survive?*

There was silence in the kitchen for a moment.

Me...because I was still trying to figure out what exactly Jett had meant by his comment.

And Jett...because he was devouring the pastry I'd put in front of him.

"Jesus, this thing is good. What is it?" Jett asked.

"It's just a simple puffed pastry with fruit and a cream cheese mixture topped with powdered sugar."

He pointed to the half empty dish as he said, "There's nothing simple about this dessert. It's fucking amazing."

I wanted to address what he'd said about me rejecting him, but it was the first easy conversation we'd had in a few days, and I didn't want to ruin it. "I could do a lot better, but I don't have everything I need for complicated stuff."

"I'll get you anything you want in Seattle if you can keep making these," he said right before he swallowed the rest of the sweet treat.

I smiled at him. "I love to bake. I'll make whatever you want. Even if you have a small kitchen, I can still do a lot with the right ingredients and a few other pans and accessories."

He dropped his fork on the empty plate and picked up the mug of coffee I'd given him before I'd dropped off the dessert. I truly believed that pastry was best with a fresh cup of coffee.

He set the mug back in place once he'd downed half of it. "My kitchen isn't exactly small," Jett said in a careful voice.

I hadn't meant to insult him in any way. "Seattle is expensive. I was researching since I'm moving there and the average rent for a one-bedroom is over two thousand dollars. I'm sure the average person doesn't have a chef's kitchen or anything elaborate."

He looked at me with a guilty expression. "I'm not exactly an average person," he stated.

I folded my arms, wondering if he was going to start gloating about what a great tech guy he was again. "Then what are you?"

His eyes were intensely focused on me as he said, "I have a chef's kitchen, Ruby. I have a downtown penthouse that's built on two levels and bigger than most houses in Seattle. I have an up-close-and-personal view of the Space Needle out some windows, and the Puget Sound from the others."

I looked at him in confusion. "But that has to be a seven-figure home. I didn't know your business was *that* big."

"It's an eight-figure home, and I can easily afford it."

"What are you trying to say?" I knew Jett wasn't delusional, but I was confused.

"Ruby, what kind of computer did I buy you?" he asked in a careful tone.

"A Lawson," I answered obligingly. "One of the best laptops on the market, according to almost all sources."

"It *is* the best," he said gruffly. "I should know because my two brothers and I own the company. Me, my brother Carter, and my brother Mason are partners and the owners of Lawson Technologies."

My brain tried to process what he was telling me, and my mind balked. Yeah, his last name *was* Lawson, but that last name was fairly common. But if he was one of the owners of Lawson Technologies, he'd be one of the richest men in the world. Lawson was an international tech company, and one of the giants.

I racked my brain for any information I had retained in my memory about the company. I didn't know much about Lawson, but I did remember reading that one of the headquarters was in Seattle.

"You're really one of *those* Lawsons?" I squeaked.

He nodded, not taking his eyes away from my face.

"Then you're one of the richest guys in the world?" I asked.

He nodded again.

"Why didn't you tell me?" I questioned, feeling a little hurt that he hadn't told me *everything*. Being a *Lawson* of *Lawson Technologies* was a pretty big deal.

He shrugged. "I guess I wanted you to like me *without* the billionaire stuff."

"I'd *like* you either way," I informed him. "You're a pretty likable guy. But it kind of freaks me out that you're *that* rich. And it hurts that you thought that I was that superficial."

"I don't," he explained. "That was how I felt in the very beginning, and after that, it really didn't seem to matter. I'm sorry. I should have told you earlier."

I glared at him. "I would have felt a lot better knowing I hadn't put you into a difficult situation when you'd shelled out so much money for me. Not that it would have changed the fact that I owe you, but

I wouldn't have felt quite as guilty if I'd known that you were going to be okay without it until I could pay you back. I was afraid I'd left you with no savings."

"I told you it wouldn't break me," he argued.

"I thought you were just being nice," I admitted.

He grinned at me, the cocky grin I hadn't seen in the last few days. "Do I have to apologize because I'm really, really rich?"

I folded my arms in front of me. "I suppose not. You already said you were sorry that you didn't tell me earlier."

I thought about some of the things he'd said, and it all made sense now, including his claim of being the best cybersecurity guy in the world. Since he owned *Lawson,* and they were known as *the best,* then his claim was definitely valid.

I felt a little silly that I hadn't put all the facts together earlier, but who expected a guy as influential as Jett to be on a rescue mission?

Okay, maybe that wasn't fair, but most guys like him were schmoozing with other rich guys, not helping the homeless personally.

"Does it really matter?" he asked.

I thought for a minute. *Did it make a difference about how I felt about Jett?*

After careful consideration, I decided it really didn't matter. But it was nice to know that helping me didn't break him.

I shook my head. "Not to me. But I'm guessing I'll get a room with a view in Seattle?" I joked.

He nodded with a relieved expression. "Best views in the city," he admitted. "Am I forgiven, then?"

I shrugged. "I'll let you know. I'm still trying to absorb the fact that I'm hanging out with one of the richest guys in existence."

"You'll get used to it," Jett answered gravely.

"What's it like in Seattle? Does it really rain all the time?"

Jett looked pretty happy that I'd changed the subject. "No. It's overcast most of the winter, but it only rains about fifty percent of the time," he answered with humor in his voice. "The traffic is horrible, but the food is fantastic, especially if you like seafood. And if you're a coffee lover, you'll find a coffee shop almost anywhere in the city. It has plenty of water and there are mountains on the opposite side of the city, so it's good for almost any kind of activity you want."

"Do you like it there?"

"I do," he admitted. "It's different from living in Colorado, but Seattle has a life of its own, and there are computer nerds everywhere."

I laughed. "So you fit right in," I teased.

He shrugged. "Pretty much."

I stood and started collecting dishes. Jett got up to help just like he always did.

Honestly, Jett seemed pretty normal for a man who had so much money. Maybe that was why I never really connected the dots with him.

As I loaded the dishwasher, I tried to wrap my head around the fact that I'd been staying with one of the most influential business-men in world.

But I couldn't see him as anything but...Jett. Since I'd known his character before I'd known about his wealth, it really didn't matter that he had more money than God.

After I'd started the dishwasher, I turned around and met Jett's beautiful green-eyed gaze, and realized that what he'd just told me didn't make a difference at all in how I felt about him. He was just as gorgeous as a billionaire as he had been as a small business owner.

He was still the same Jett who had done everything he could to help me. The same nice guy I was starting to trust more and more every day.

And he was *still* the man who had kissed me like he really wanted me.

I'm going to have to set him straight about what happened when he kissed me.

I knew that I was going to have to tell him what had *really* caused me to freak out.

And it would be one of the hardest things I'd ever had to do.

Chapter 11

Jett

The next morning, I hung up the phone with a sinking feeling in my chest.

I had news that I had to tell Ruby, but I wondered what kind of price she'd pay for hearing it.

I shoved my cell back into my pocket, and left my bedroom where my bags were being loaded for our departure to Seattle.

I stopped in the hallway as I saw Ruby tugging her suitcase out of her room, which would have amused me on any other day since I'd told her to let the valet pick it up.

But today wasn't *any other day.*

"Leave it," I told Ruby as I took her hand. "We have to talk."

She gave me a questioning gaze, but left the suitcase in the hall to follow me.

The connection that Ruby and I had was strange to me, but not unwelcome. She always seemed to sense my mood, and had an uncanny way to judging when to say something and when not to argue based on my expression.

"What's wrong?" she said as we rode the elevator to the ground floor.

"Nothing is exactly *wrong*," I hedged.

Jesus! The last thing I wanted was to talk about her past again, but it was unavoidable.

"We need to stop in Ohio, Ruby. Or we will if you want to recover your inheritance." I hoped to hell she'd say she trusted me to take care of her so she didn't have to deal with this right now, but it wasn't fair for her to be cheated out of anything she deserved.

"I didn't inherit anything," she said as we arrived in the kitchen.

"Your uncle is dead, Ruby. He died of a heart attack a couple of months ago. Apparently, your mom and dad *did* have life insurance and you were the sole beneficiary. When your parents died, your uncle had to put it in a trust for you. The only things that were ever claimed from the account were some small costs from your high school. He couldn't touch it for anything else, and it was yours when you turned twenty-one." I tried to explain as briefly as possible so she didn't have to digest very much at one time.

I watched as her expression changed from confusion to recognition, and then finally went completely blank. "He lied," she said stoically. "He told me I was a burden to him, and that I was lucky to have a roof over my head. He said my parents hadn't cared what happened to me, and that they wanted me to fend for myself because I was a burden to them, too, and I made them even poorer. He actually said he'd had to pay their debts."

"He lied," I replied.

My gut ached with the desire to get vengeance for her, but I couldn't. The only thing I could do was help her pick up the pieces after her uncle had destroyed her even before she'd been old enough to walk away.

I'd been searching for the bastard since I'd first met Ruby. When his niece had run away, he'd moved to the other side of Ohio, but some of my personal team had finally dug up the information that he'd died and had been brought back to his home town to be buried in the same cemetery as Ruby's parents.

His estate was up in the air since there were no immediate relatives, but Ruby's uncle hadn't really had very much to settle after he'd been buried. Mostly just the money that had been left in trust for Ruby.

"How much?" she asked.

"Two hundred and fifty thousand was paid out," I told her. "He managed to claim some for your food and living expenses. But most of it is still in trust."

Even though Ruby's parents *had* been tight on money, they'd always made sure their only daughter was protected since they didn't have a lot of family. They'd obviously wanted her to be taken care of if they weren't around to do it themselves.

In reality, they'd obviously put their daughter's safety over their own comfort.

"What do we have to do in Ohio?" she asked, her expression still unreadable.

"You're going to need to sign some paperwork to get your trust," I explained.

She nodded. "Then I guess we're going to Ohio."

"Are you okay?" I asked, worried that she hadn't really said much.

"I will be," she answered vaguely.

I expedited things so we could get in and out of Ohio quickly. There was nothing there for Ruby anymore, but she was going to have to deal with her past one more time.

While we were on our way to the airport, I swore that *this* time would be the last.

"I'm glad it's over," Ruby said in the same monotone voice she'd used all day.

She was actually starting to scare me.

She'd signed the paperwork involving her trust like it was just another task she had to complete, asking the necessary questions with very little emotion.

We were in the car I'd rented, and we were headed back to the airport after going through everything with an attorney who had taken on the task of getting Ruby's trust to her bank account.

She still had very little to say. Her words had been her first since we'd gotten back into the vehicle I was now driving.

"Can you turn left up here?" she asked.

It was a small town, and we were approaching the edge of the city limits. It wasn't difficult for me to make the sudden adjustments to make the requested direction.

She moved forward in her seat, her expression pensive for a moment before she said, "I think it's the next right."

I knew exactly where she was going, and I'd anticipated the instructions. I had come to know Ruby pretty well, so I knew she wasn't going to leave town without visiting her parents.

"I know where the cemetery is," I told her soberly, making it unnecessary for her to keep trying to guide me to where she wanted to go.

I also understood her need to find a way to make a connection. I hadn't gone to see my parents' resting place for some time, but I'd flown back to Rocky Springs fairly often to visit my parents' graves for the first several years after their deaths.

Once we passed through the gates, she guided me straight to the site, and then jumped out of the car.

I met her on the passenger side of the vehicle.

"I wish I would have brought some flowers or something," she said in a wistful tone.

Clasping her hand, I answered, "I took the liberty. I hope you don't mind."

We walked together silently to the place where Ruby's parents had been put to rest. I wasn't exactly sure of the spot, but I'd arranged for flowers to be put on their stone.

I stopped when Ruby halted next to me. "This is it," she informed me as she looked down at the single stone that marked the site.

"I'd wanted a lot more for them, but my uncle said it was all he could afford," she murmured.

I squeezed her hand. "He didn't pay for this, Ruby. It came out of the life insurance before it was put into your trust. But your parents had everything laid out in the will. They didn't want a big stone. All they wanted was for you to be well if something happened."

"They were like that," she said, her voice starting to tremble with emotion. "Neither one of them ever wanted much except to be together."

"That's all they wanted, even after their death," I said solemnly.

"I hate my uncle for making me second-guess how much they loved me," she stated. "They were everything to me. They were all I had. But he told me they had never really wanted me, and I had spoiled their opportunities for a better life. He made me rethink everything I knew was true. And I believed it because he'd forced me to listen to him. And I guess after a while, you start to believe it if you hear it enough times."

I squeezed her hand again, but my gut was rolling with fury. "They knew you loved them, Ruby. I know they did. You loved them even when you weren't quite sure if they loved you."

"But they did love me, Jett. They did. But I believed everything bad that my uncle said about them."

I turned her toward me and grasped her shoulders. "No, you didn't," I growled. "In your heart, you always knew the truth. But there's no way you couldn't have had your doubts when crap was being pounded into your head every damn day. You were a kid, Ruby, a teenager who had lost the two people you loved the most. Give yourself a damn break. Your parents would have understood."

She looked up at me with her liquid dark eyes, and it broke my damn heart to see the turbulence in their depths.

"They loved me, Jett. They always loved me, and my uncle was just...evil. But they had no way of knowing that because he didn't show that part of himself to them."

I nodded, relieved that she was finally seeing the truth.

"Oh, God," she said as she stared back at me.

I gathered the broken woman into my arms as she did something I'd never seen before.

She started sobbing against my shoulder, crying like she'd never stop.

I held her against me, comforting her in her grief, recognizing Ruby Kent finally trusted me, even if she didn't know it yet.

Chapter 12

Ruby

"Jett, this is incredible," I said in a breathless voice as I dropped my small purse on a chair in the living room.

My first glance at Jett's high-rise penthouse had left me stunned.

I'd started to come to terms with his enormous wealth, first on the flight to Ohio, and then to Seattle on his private jet, but the penthouse pretty much blew me away.

Jett leaned a hip against the kitchen counter and watched me flit around the enormous living room as he said, "I thought material things didn't mean much to you."

I knew he was teasing. His voice was thick with amusement.

I finally plopped down in a window seat that had a perfect view of the top part of the Space Needle. The penthouse was slightly higher, but it almost looked framed in the window like a picture.

But it was all too real.

"I'm not materialistic," I argued. "But there's no way I *can't* be impressed by the way the architect designed this place, or the fantastic views."

I got up and wandered to another large window with a seat and looked at the water. "Is that Puget Sound?"

We were sitting at the top of an incline, so we looked down at sweeping water views.

"Technically, it's probably Elliott Bay, but it's still part of the Sound."

"Can we get closer?" I asked excitedly.

"Why do we need to get closer? You can see it from here."

"I wasn't even close to water when I was a kid. And once I got south, I rarely went near the beaches."

I'd tried to keep my head low and stay out of trouble in Miami. Unfortunately, I'd *still* fallen for the lies of human traffickers.

Jett chuckled. "There's a seafood restaurant on a pier not far from here. We can go check it out tomorrow night. You can't get much closer to the water without swimming."

I beamed at him, relieved that our relationship was friendly again.

Coping with the revelations about my parents, and the fact that I'd been lied to by my uncle, hadn't been easy, but Jett had been so supportive that it helped. After I'd cried all over him in the cemetery, we'd talked about some happy memories I'd had with my parents, and we'd fallen into an easy comradery that I'd missed.

I wouldn't see my inheritance for a while, not until all the legal stuff was done. But at least I knew that my folks had provided for my future, and that I wasn't completely dependent on anyone.

I turned and stood, crossing my arms as I said, "That means you're paying for *another* dinner."

He nodded, his eyes dancing with humor as he answered, "Makes sense since you don't have any money yet." He lifted his hand to stop me from speaking. "And before you start arguing, you can cook the day after tomorrow, and that's much more than payback for any restaurant we visit. Especially if you make those incredible pastries. I can't cook worth a damn, so you'll be saving me money, and we can call it even. Can we agree on that? I'd like to show you Seattle, maybe even get out of the city and check out the wineries and the mountains. But I don't want to fight every time I pay."

I lowered my head, purposely losing eye contact with him. I wanted to be with him. I wanted to see the Northwest so badly. "I'm sorry. I just feel so bad because you always have to pay. For everything. It will be nice when I can actually afford to pay you back, and have something to see me through until I can find a job."

"It won't be forever," he said gruffly. "You'll get on your feet once everything is settled in Ohio. Just let yourself be Cinderella for a while. You deserve that, Ruby."

I gave him a dubious look, but didn't say anything.

"So you're going to accept the fact that I'm going to pay for stuff?" he asked.

"If you agree to let me cook most of the time." I nodded my head toward the kitchen. "I can't wait to get into that spectacular kitchen."

"Done," he said quickly, then moved forward to pick up my suitcase. "Let me show you the bedrooms and you can pick your favorite."

I followed him, knowing that the rest of the suitcases were being brought up by a valet.

We took an elevator to the second level, an extravagance I was glad that Jett had available because of his knee.

I took a beautiful room accented in light blue, and with gorgeous views of the water.

"I'll unpack and then I can fix dinner," I told him as I motioned for him to drop the suitcase on the king-sized bed.

"You can let my assistant unpack," he corrected. "And we can order pizza. It's been a long day."

My eyes shot up to his face. "You have an assistant already?"

I'd thought I was going to be his assistant.

He grinned. "I have several of them. But you're the only one who's going to live here."

I rolled my eyes at him. "So you didn't actually desperately need my help or anything."

His expression grew intense as he looked at me from the top of my head to my feet, showing no sign of what he was thinking.

Finally, he said, "I needed *you.*"

A spark caught fire in my belly as I met his earnest gaze, unable to look away. I needed *him*, too, in a way I couldn't really explain with words. I wanted to throw myself into his arms and beg his forgiveness for messing up the only opportunity I'd had to get closer to him.

Earlier, he'd been a friend and a shoulder to cry on when I needed it. But I wanted so much more.

I regretted running away from him in a stupid panic, but it had been a reaction I hadn't been able to stifle.

Not then.

And probably not now if I didn't approach things differently.

But I still *wanted* to touch him. I craved a connection with Jett, something much more intimate than what was happening between us now.

I stepped forward and put a gentle kiss on his cheek. "Thank you," I murmured as I moved back. "Thank you for everything you've done for me."

His fists were clenched to his side as he answered, "You're welcome, Cinderella."

Jett turned and left the room like his ass was on fire, and I knew it was because he wasn't comfortable being physically close to me anymore. Not unless I was sobbing my heart out on his shoulder. I'd flipped out on him once before, and he was apparently wary.

I couldn't exactly blame him.

"Here we go," a female voice said from the bedroom door. "Your suitcases."

Our driver and a well-dressed older woman entered my bedroom. Their efficiency was impressive. I watched as the lady pulled a few suitcase holders from the closet, and the driver placed the suitcases on them before he left the room, presumably to deliver Jett's suitcases to his bedroom.

I stepped forward as the female started to open the first of two suitcases. "I can do that," I said, feeling flustered because somebody actually thought they needed to unpack for me.

"Oh, no, dear," the woman said in an admonishing voice that made me feel like a two-year-old. "Mr. Lawson specifically asked me to do it for you."

"I'm Ruby," I told her. "And I always unpack my own things."

She smiled at me patiently, and nodded her head. "It's very nice to meet you, Ruby. I'm Shirley, Mr. Lawson's executive assistant, and he pays me well to unpack things for him and his guests."

She was nice, but adamant, and I didn't want to get off on the wrong foot with somebody who worked so closely with Jett.

As she opened the suitcase, I snatched up my underwear. "Can I at least put away my undies?" I asked.

I didn't have anything particularly sexy, but it just seemed all wrong to let somebody else handle my lingerie.

"Of course. You can help all you want, and let me know where you want your things," she said cheerfully.

"Honestly, I really don't know," I confided. "I've never been here before."

"It's a lovely home," she shared as she hung the items Jett had bought for me, most of which I hadn't even worn. "I think you'll be comfortable here."

How in the world could I *not* be comfortable in a multimillion dollar home like Jett's? "I'm sure I will," I answered. "How long have you worked for Jett?"

"Been with him for the last five years," Shirley answered as she handed me the hung-up clothes to put in the closet when I stepped forward. "Like you, I don't think he wanted anybody to touch his underwear, either, but he finally got too busy to do everything himself."

A laugh escaped from my mouth. Shirley was matter-of-fact and professional, and I liked her rather dry sense of humor. "He's a busy guy. He needs somebody to put his clothes away, I suppose," I told her.

"Best boss I've ever had, and I've had quite a few. All three of the Lawson boys are good people."

I smirked because I wasn't sure how Jett would react to being called *a boy*.

"So you knew him before he was injured?" I was curious how much Jett's accident had changed him. "What was he like *before* it happened?"

Shirley was storing the suitcases in another closet as she answered, "He was always the most sensitive brother, and his personality is still the same. But his spirit seemed to be broken after his fiancée tossed him aside. That one was never going to make him happy. And he's *lucky* she left him, but it hurt to watch a man as gravely injured as Mr. Lawson have to take another blow after the accident. His spirit had taken enough of a beating."

"How long did it take him to get his spirit *back*?" I questioned.

"I'm not sure that he really did," she said thoughtfully. "Oh, I have no doubt he realizes that he made a lucky escape, and he wouldn't get near the fiancée who hurt him again, but he's…changed. He doesn't laugh much anymore, and she shattered some of his confidence."

"Unless it has to do with his computer skills," I corrected. "He's still pretty cocky about those."

Shirley chuckled as she walked toward the door. "He has a right to be. Have a good night, Ruby. I'm sure we'll run into each other again soon."

"Thank you, Shirley," I called out as she left the room.

I sat down on the bed, thinking.

Since I hadn't known Jett before his accident, I had no way of knowing if Jett had lost something he couldn't regain.

His confidence?

His self-worth?

Since I'd never had much of those things myself, I probably wasn't the best person to help him get them back.

But because Jett deserved to be happy, I was willing to give it my best shot.

Chapter 13

Ruby

All I want is to look nice.

I lamented over this simple fact the following day because I knew Jett was taking me out to a waterfront restaurant, and I really didn't want to wear jeans.

Seattle was Jett's city, and he obviously knew a lot of people here. The last thing I wanted was to run into somebody influential with Jett while I still looked like a homeless woman.

Yeah, I didn't smell bad now, and my body and clothes were clean, but I wasn't the type of woman who would normally be seen with a billionaire.

Not that I was putting myself down, because I was learning how *not* to feel inferior to people who had more money than I did—which had been pretty much everybody before I'd learned about my inheritance.

But sometimes, I just wanted to feel *normal*. I wanted to look good just for myself. Okay, and *maybe* for Jett.

Because of my sessions with Annette, I was starting to believe that I was worthy of self-care and doing things just because I wanted to do them.

I might be hesitant to reach out and grab what I wanted, but I was starting to think that I deserved the things I'd never had.

I stepped off the elevator at the ground floor and looked around for Jett's driver.

He ended up *finding me.*

"Ms. Kent?"

I turned around and saw the face connected to the voice that was calling my name.

He was a very distinguished looking, silver-haired gentleman in an elegant suit and tie.

"Please call me Ruby," I requested as I put my hand out to him. "I really appreciate this."

I'd spent the morning helping Jett get his office organized after so much time away. Then, I'd asked him if I could use his car and driver since I didn't have a valid license yet.

I think he'd assumed I wanted to see the sights, and he offered to go with me, but I'd told him I'd really like some time alone.

He'd capitulated immediately, and though he'd looked disappointed, Jett had hooked me up to meet his driver in the lobby.

I didn't plan on sightseeing, but the afternoon was for me.

I'd debated over what outfit to wear, but I'd finally admitted to myself none of them were really my style. They were way too fussy, and I hadn't felt comfortable in any of the garments even though I'd tried on every single dress in the wardrobe Jett had given me.

I told myself it was a waste to buy another dress, but my self-talk hadn't worked. I wanted a dress that was *me*, and I wanted to choose it myself.

"You can call me Pete," the gentleman said as he shook my hand politely. "You have no reason to appreciate the fact that I'm doing my job," he said genially.

I shrugged. "Sorry, but I still do appreciate it," I answered with a smile. "You're paid to haul Jett around."

I frowned as I pulled my hand back, noticing how ragged and torn up my hands and nails looked.

"And anyone he tells me to haul around," Pete added with a smile. "Where are we going today?"

I searched in my cross-body purse, and finally found what I was looking for. "I need to get to one of these banks, if you know where they have one." I flipped the savings book for him to see. "I don't have the right dress, and Jett is going to take me to a restaurant on the water tonight. I have to take some money out."

He nodded. "There's one not far from here. I'll take you there."

I followed him as we went outside and he opened the back door of a luxury sedan.

The vehicle had to be custom. The back was outfitted with a huge space where you could do almost anything in the vehicle, from having a drink to taking a nap.

"Can I sit in the front with you?" I asked hesitantly. "I'm not really used to all this. I just wanted a ride."

"That's not usually done," he mused.

I folded my arms and gave him a skeptical look. "Are you trying to tell me that Jett doesn't sit in the front? He's not exactly a guy who always follows the rules."

Pete cracked a little smile. "Sometimes he does keep me company up front," he admitted as he closed the back door and opened the front passenger side.

I hopped in with a sigh of relief. For me, there was just something wrong with having a driver and sitting alone in the backseat.

As Pete took his place behind the wheel, he said, "You seem to know Mr. Lawson quite well."

"Well enough to figure out that he wouldn't leave you alone up here unless he had urgent things to accomplish. He's fairly down-to-earth for a rich guy."

"To be honest, he usually prefers to drive himself unless his leg is bothering him."

I nodded. "That sounds like him."

We pulled into the parking lot of the bank soon after we'd left Jett's penthouse.

After promising Pete I'd try to hurry and hearing him tell me that I had to do no such thing, I jogged into the bank and stood in line for a teller.

When it was my turn, I stepped up to speak with the cheerful blonde woman who was smiling at me.

"I need to make a withdrawal please," I said breathlessly.

She took my account book from my hand and entered the account number.

"How much would you like to withdraw?" she asked politely while she appeared to wait for the account information to come up.

"Do you know how much it would be for a good haircut, manicure, a little bit of makeup, and a dress that's appropriate for a waterfront dinner?" I asked. Okay, so maybe it was an odd question to ask, but it was better to be weird than completely ignorant. If I wanted to get around in Seattle and make a new life for myself, I had to acclimate to my environment. I wasn't living on the streets anymore, and my situation was far from hopeless now—thanks to my parents.

"I know a great place for makeovers where they let you try the makeup first before you buy," she said with animated enthusiasm. "And they do hair, pedicures, and manicures. You can have an entire makeover for one fairly reasonable price."

The thought of reinventing myself to some extent was appealing.

I hadn't really wanted to use the emergency money that Jett had deposited, but I definitely hadn't wanted to ask him for money, even though I knew he'd happily give it to me.

I figured if I used some money from the savings account, I could just replace it once I got my inheritance and started working. There was no way Jett was going to take his money back out of my account anyway. Not unless I had something there that was mine.

"Do I have enough in my account to cover the makeover?" I asked hopefully.

The woman finally focused on the screen. Her eyes kept assessing the account, and I was starting to fear that something was wrong.

Maybe there was nothing in the account.
Maybe the bank had screwed up Jett's deposit.
Maybe there would be no makeover for me.

My shoulders slumped in disappointment. It wasn't the end of the world, but it was the first bold step I'd taken in my life, and it looked like it was about to blow up in my face.

"Would you like your balance?" she asked.

"Yes, please," I answered.

"Can I see your ID? It says here that you'll probably have an expired Ohio driver's license until you obtain a valid driver's license for Washington."

I rifled through my bag and took out my ID. "It's still Ohio."

Jett must have given the bank instructions and information, so he'd obviously intended to leave some money in the account.

He'd already done so much for me that it didn't matter whether or not I could buy a dress. I'd just hoped for some kind of change, a symbolic gesture that I was going to get a normal life, and come out of counseling as a healthier person.

I'd never had a real haircut, much less a makeover to see how I would look when I went to the effort of looking my best. My mother had always trimmed my thick, dark hair when I was younger, and I'd had far more important things to worry about when I was alone and on the streets.

I'd never owned a nice dress, or something that was in style. I knew I had a closet full of them now thanks to Jett, but I hadn't *chosen* them. And I finally wanted to be exactly who I was, and embrace my new life.

Once I paid Jett back for the money he'd spent on the auction, I knew I wasn't going to be wealthy. But I'd have enough to make sure I was never homeless again.

Nobody would ever look at me and call me beautiful.

But maybe I was hoping that Jett would look at me with lust in his eyes, the same kind of desire I felt when I looked at him.

The teller took a pen and a small piece of blank paper to write down my balance and slide it across the counter as she said, "You can get as many makeovers as you want," she said.

I looked down at the balance. My stomach lurched and my knees threatened to give out as I saw all of those *zeros*.

Jett truly *had* wanted me to be taken care of if anything ever happened to him.

He'd given me more than just emergency money.

The account that had been drawn down to nothing when I'd left Ohio now had a balance of just over two million dollars.

My fairy tale was getting a whole lot crazier, and my Cinderella moniker was starting to fit me perfectly.

I didn't know if I should feel horrified or happy, but I pushed that to the back of my mind to ponder later.

I drew out enough money to cover what I needed, and some extra so I could pick up the things I needed to make Jett a ton of pastries.

My body was still shaking as I hopped back into the car.

"Are you all right, Ms. Ruby?" Pete asked as I fumbled with my seat belt.

I was way too flustered to tell him he didn't need to be formal with my name. It took all I had just to fasten the buckle of the belt.

"No, I'm *not* really okay," I blurted out. "I *was* homeless, and now I have more money in my bank account than I'd probably see there after a lifetime of working several jobs. Not to mention that my parents set me up to be okay after they died, so I have more money coming in."

"And that's a bad thing?" Pete asked, sounding confused.

"It's not *my money* in the bank right now, Pete. I didn't earn it. It's Jett's."

He turned his head, not yet moving the vehicle as he looked at me. "If it's in your account, it's now yours," he mused.

"I can *never* take the money. Jett has already helped me so much. You have no idea," I said frantically.

"I think I *might* have a very good idea," he contradicted. "Mr. Lawson has helped many people, me included," he confided.

I turned my head sharply to look at him. "What do you mean?"

"You said you were homeless?"

I nodded slowly.

"So was I at one time," he shared. "Years ago, I lost my wife and my three children in an accident. I went from a man who had everything to a man who had nothing to live for. I didn't care what happened to me. I drank to kill the pain, and I eventually ended up on the streets."

"Oh, my God," I gasped. "I'm so sorry."

"Thank you, Ms. Ruby, but I'm better now. I met Mr. Lawson at a bar. I'd gotten some money begging, and I went straight into a pub to get a drink since I was in withdrawal. And even though I looked like a derelict, Mr. Lawson still struck up a conversation with me. To this day, I couldn't tell you why I dumped all of my woes on a man I'd just met, but he listened carefully before he made me a deal."

"What?" I asked, so fascinated by his story that I couldn't say anything else.

"If I got myself together and went through rehab successfully, he'd make sure that I had a job, a roof over my head again, and enough money to survive the rest of my life. Only a fool would refuse an offer like that. And even though I'd done some stupid things, I was no fool."

"And you obviously made it," I commented.

"That I did, and then some. I think I was ready to deal with my grief, but by that time, there was nobody there except for Mr. Lawson. So I worked hard to get clean, and then I worked hard for him. He helped me sort through all of the legal things that had to be worked out with life insurance and settlements from the trucking company that had killed my family. I was well beyond set for life, but Mr. Lawson refused any kind of repayment for my rehab and all my other expenses that I racked up until all the legal issues were done."

"Is that why you're still working?" I asked, knowing how stubborn Jett could be about getting paid back.

Pete shook his head. "Not at all. Do you really think Mr. Lawson would ever let me work without drawing a paycheck?"

"Then why are you still working?"

"Maybe I'm just hoping that someday, in some way, I'll get the opportunity to help him out like he helped me. Maybe not with money because Lord knows he has more money than almost anybody else in the world. But money isn't everything. He *wants* me to retire and enjoy my life. But I'm fine with waiting for a chance to help him, and keeping busy. My lovely wife of one year is still working, so I'd be bored if I retired anyway."

I smiled at him. "You got married again?"

"I did. And she's a good woman. Life goes on, even when we don't necessarily want it to, and sometimes we just have to catch up with it when we're done grieving."

I nodded hard. I remembered the day I'd lost my own family, and wondering why everything stayed the same when my world was falling apart. "So I'm not Jett's only stray that he's rescued?" I asked.

"No, Ms. Ruby. And he doesn't see us as anything less than he is. He just considers it his way of giving back because he has so much."

"I know," I acknowledged. Jett had never made me feel like *less than* because I needed help. "But I've always had a difficult time taking anything from him."

"Because you're a good person," Pete observed. "But let him take care of you right now while you're fragile. You can give back later, once you have everything together. I'm personally involved with helping some homeless projects with fundraising and volunteer work."

"Can I help?" I asked, eager to help others who were still in my former position.

He beamed at me. "Not now. But I'd welcome your help in the future. You have to look to yourself first. You can't help somebody else unless you can take care of yourself first."

"In that case, can you help me find an inexpensive place to buy a dress? Jett is taking me out to eat on the waterfront tonight. And I'd like to not look like a vagabond," I joked.

He winked at me. "I know a place. I'm one of the few people who actually grew up in this city. I have lots of connections."

I laughed, feeling better than I had since the day Jett had rescued me.

Pete was right. I *did* need to get myself together, and that needed to be my focus for now. I was progressing slowly with counseling. I had an appointment to get my driver's license and my GED so I could decide what I wanted to do in the future.

Because of Jett, I was going to succeed.

If nothing else, I was going to let him know that I'd been worth saving.

Chapter 14

Ruby

"I look…okay," I whispered to myself uncertainly as I stood in front of the mirror in my bedroom suite.

I hadn't seen Jett yet, but he'd bellowed out from his office that our reservation was at seven p.m. as I'd come back into the penthouse.

I was ready, and it was barely six fifteen. But I knew traffic was probably going to be crazy.

As I peered into the mirror again, I finally saw the woman I could be if I was able to take care of myself.

The stylist had taken off a considerable amount of length from my dark hair to shape it into a healthier style. It barely brushed my shoulders now, but the big fat curls she'd put into my normally straight hair made me look older, and more sophisticated. And the reddish-brown highlighting made my hair shine.

My skin was glowing from the makeup the makeover artist had used sparingly by my request.

I didn't want to *change* my appearance; I wanted to *enhance* what was already there.

She'd highlighted my dark eyes with a smoky-colored shadow that made my boring, brown eyes a little more mysterious.

Pete had taken me to the store where his wife worked, and I'd chosen a dress that had been on clearance because summer was coming to an end. It was the first days of fall, but the weather was still warm enough to wear a summer outfit, so I'd purchased the beautiful dress, knowing I could always wear it next year if the weather got chilly soon.

I'd fallen in love with the simplicity of the little black dress almost immediately. It was strapless, which was going to take some getting used to, but I loved the slightly asymmetrical look. The front, which ended just above the knee, was slightly shorter than the back, and that small difference made the silky material fall around my body in an unusual and elegant shape.

I twirled around, loving the way the skirt fell right back into place when I stopped.

Maybe the dress would be nothing special to most women, but it was special to me because it was the first dress I'd ever chosen myself.

A sharp rap on the door brought me out of my fantasy. "Hey, Cinderella. You ready?" Jett called through the door.

"On my way," I answered as I slipped my feet into a pair of sandals. I'd picked up a black pair with low heels so I didn't make a fool out of myself by tripping over stilettos.

I picked up my purse, and frowned. I knew it wasn't exactly a dress purse. It was the same small, black, cross-body that I used every day, but it would have to work.

I took a deep breath, and left my room, making my way to the living room downstairs where I knew Jett would be waiting.

He was seated on the couch with his phone, apparently answering text messages, judging by the way he was typing furiously with his head down.

My heart skittered as I realized he was wearing a beautiful dark suit with a green and charcoal colored tie. Jett was the kind of guy who could own anything he was wearing. He looked just as comfortable in a suit as he did in a pair of jeans, and I was pretty sure the green in the tie would match his eyes.

I froze as he finally looked up and saw me, noticing that I'd been right. The gorgeous green in his tie really did match his eyes.

He dropped his phone in his pocket, and then got up slowly, his intense stare never leaving me as he stood.

"What in the hell did you do?" he said gutturally.

"You don't like it," I said as I finally moved, my shoulders slumping as I moved toward him. "I was trying something new, something that looked nicer than jeans, but less fussy than what I have in my wardrobe," I added, trying to sound upbeat when I actually felt crushed.

He reached out and fingered a fat curl as I stopped in front of him. "Mission accomplished," he said in a low, sexy baritone. " You look stunning, Ruby."

"But?" I questioned, knowing something wasn't right.

"But I'll be fighting every guy who so much as looks at you," he said in a husky tone. "Because I'll know that when they look at all that beautiful skin you're showing, they'll be thinking about getting you naked."

My heart thumped against my chest wall, and my body started to tremble as he ran a finger along my bare shoulder.

"The only guy I want to notice me is you," I said breathlessly. "I wanted you to be proud of the woman you're with. I tried on everything in my wardrobe, but none of them felt like me."

He tipped my chin up so our eyes connected. "I've *always* noticed you," he said firmly. "And you've *always* been beautiful. But tonight—you take my breath away. And I should have known better than to try to buy you clothes. I can send them all back."

I sighed as I fell into his beautiful eyes, unable to look away. "I was afraid you didn't like the new look. Not that I'm going to look this way every day," I said hurriedly. "I'm not a fussy kind of female. But I did like the manicure. My nails were a mess."

He took a lock of my hair between his fingers. "And what did they do to your hair?"

"They had to cut it to get it healthy again. All my ends were split and dry."

"I'll pay for all of this, Ruby. I should have thought about it before now," he said regretfully.

I smiled at him. "You *did* pay for it. I had to take money from my savings. But I'll put it back. And we need to talk about you putting that kind of money into my savings account," I informed him. "I nearly had heart failure."

"Not tonight," he said hoarsely, his eyes still glued to me. "I'm going to have the most beautiful woman in the world on my arm. I want to savor that."

I fake punched him in the upper arm. "Okay, now it's getting pretty thick," I teased. "But I'm glad you think I look acceptable. It's nice to feel like a woman for once."

"You need a coat," he said. "We'll be on the water."

"I didn't quite get that far," I confessed. "And I definitely didn't need one in Miami."

"I have some female stuff in the last bedroom at the very end of the hallway upstairs. But I'm not sure if she left a coat," he said thoughtfully.

"I refuse to wear anything that bitch left here," I said before I could censor my words.

But I wasn't at all sorry I said them. I'd rather freeze than wear anything that Jett's ex had worn with him.

He took my hand and tugged me toward the elevator. "I don't think *Dani* is really a bitch. But my sister definitely has her moments." He punched the elevator button once we were safely inside.

"Oh, God. I'm sorry. I guess I immediately thought about..." My voice trailed off in embarrassment.

He was grinning at me. "My kitten has claws," he drawled.

"I don't like what she did to you," I said firmly.

He leaned closer. "Are you trying to protect me, Ruby?"

I frowned at him. "So what if I am?"

He took a deep breath before he said, "I think I might like it." He paused before he said, "Fuck! What is that scent? It smells like sugar cookies or vanilla."

"A fragrance I tried at the salon. I liked it. It's light and sweet, but nothing overpowering."

"It makes me want to take a bite out of you," he grumbled.

I shivered, wishing he'd go ahead and take as many bites as he liked.

As I looked at his fevered eyes, my nipples hardened in response, and my body was so hungry for him that I wanted to forget dinner and go straight to dessert here at home.

"Jett, I—"

"Don't," he interrupted as he stepped back. "I overstepped. I seem to do a hell of a lot of that when it comes to you."

His hand raked through his hair in frustration as the elevator doors opened.

He exited and led the way to the bedroom where some of Dani's belongings were apparently stored.

As he opened the closet doors, he warned, "Some of them are older than others. Her stuff always seemed to end up in my condo when she was taking off for some assignment overseas. I've collected a ton of her things. Now that she's getting married to Marcus, I'm shipping them to his place."

"She's getting married?" I said with excitement as I carefully looked through the garments and selected a gorgeous black wool coat.

He nodded.

"Does she love him?" I asked softly.

Jett took the coat from me and held it up to help me put it on. "I sure as hell hope so since they're tying the knot. She's known Marcus and all of the Colters since we were young, and I think Marcus has always been the one. It just took them awhile to realize it."

"I'm happy for her," I said sincerely. "She deserves a man who loves her."

"She wants you to come to the wedding, if you can make it," he said. "It would make her happy if you'd come with me."

"I'd like that," I told him. "If I won't be in the way."

"The Colters own an enormous resort. I think we can find room," he said drily as he took my hand and led me back to the elevator.

"I hope she doesn't mind me wearing her coat," I said.

Jett snorted as he laughed. "Cinderella, I can *guarantee* you that she doesn't even remember she has it."

"I can't imagine having *that* many clothes," I mused.

We rode down in the elevator and were out the door in moments. Jett finally said, "Funny thing is, Dani's never really been that crazy about clothes. I think she gets stuff when she needs it, but then immediately forgets about it. She pretty much wore the same stuff all the time overseas, and it definitely wasn't fancy."

Pete opened the door of the sedan as we walked outside. "Good evening," he greeted us. "You're both looking very elegant tonight."

Jett stopped before he got into the car and frowned at his driver. "Did you take Ruby around to help her get so *elegant?*" he asked Pete irritably.

The driver beamed at his boss. "I certainly did."

"I'll fire you later," Jett said in a dangerous voice.

I looked at Pete, alarmed that Jett was threatening his job.

The driver winked at me as he answered cheerily, "I think I've heard that quite a few times before, boss, and I'm still here."

"I'm doing it this time," Jett told him as he ducked into the car.

"He never does," Pete said in a low voice. "He just likes to remind me that he can."

My body relaxed as I realized this was the way the two men interacted with each other, and they both seemed to enjoy it.

I smiled at Pete as I got into the car, happy the driver wasn't going to lose his job, and that Jett had at least one other person who would always have his back, whether he wanted it or not.

Chapter 15

Jett

I wasn't a drinker, but seeing Ruby all dressed up and looking like a woman I desperately needed to take to bed had been the last straw for me.

I tossed back the last of my whiskey and signaled the waiter for another as I stared at the woman sitting across from me.

Granted, I'd wanted her from the moment I'd seen her up on a stage, being sold to the highest bidder. But other than one slip-up, I'd resisted the primal urge to make sure she was always going to belong to me in the most elemental ways I could think of, and my imagination had run pretty wild when it came to Ruby.

I'd given myself a plethora of reasons to stay away from her, and even though it hadn't been easy, those excuses had worked.

Number one, she was afraid of me and my physical appearance. It had stung for a while after she'd shied away from my scars. But maybe her reaction had been for the best.

Number two, she was young—way too young. There was nine years and a whole lot of experience between the two of us. Ruby hadn't really had any opportunity to live as an adult. She'd gone from a bad childhood to a homeless adult life. She needed time to adjust.

Number three, she was a virgin, for God's sake. What in the hell did I know about virgins?

"Are you okay?" Ruby asked tentatively.

My eyes turned toward her, something I'd been trying to avoid. Every time I looked at her, I was even more tempted to help her get used to my damn scars and convince her that she needed to be initiated into the pleasures of down and dirty sex.

Ruby's eyes were even darker and more intriguing than they'd been when she'd been onstage at the auction, and they made me think about more than just rescuing her.

I wanted to fuck her.

Bad.

But I cared about her, too. More than I wanted to admit, even to myself. "I'm good," I said with less warmth than I wanted to project.

Christ! I was losing my damn mind.

If I was really honest, I'd admit that I'd been fighting the urge to touch her ever since I'd kissed her. But I'd been using excuses one, two, or three to keep my ass in line.

Unfortunately, they weren't working all that well anymore.

Not since Ruby had reminded me tonight that even though she was young, she wasn't *that young*.

She was turning twenty-three shortly, but it wasn't her age that kept me in check.

It was the horrified look on her face when she'd ran away from me and my scarred body.

I'd wondered if I should just find myself a woman and get relief, even if I had to pay for it. But I knew damn well it wouldn't help. Ruby would be there with me every single moment, reminding me that the only one I wanted was her.

If I got myself off…she was *always* there. So I had no reason to think that she *wouldn't* be just as present if I had sex with another female.

To tell the truth, I was screwed, and I had no idea how to keep going from day to day without blowing off some steam.

So I kept getting myself off while I fantasized about a woman who had become an obsession for me.

I was pathetic.

I knew it.

But I had no idea how to stop it.

"So, I'm thinking about moving to Africa to become a game warden," Ruby said right before she took a sip of her wine.

I nodded, and swallowed the lump in my throat. "That's great," I said automatically, too caught up in her sultry eyes to make any kind of intelligent statement.

"Do you think I'd get eaten by a tiger?"

I frowned at her. "What? There are no tigers in Africa, Ruby."

Her lips formed into a smile. "I know. I was just wondering if you were ever going to come out of your coma," she said impishly.

I coughed. "I'm sorry. I wasn't paying attention."

It was rare that I wasn't fully engaged in a conversation with Ruby. But I'd been losing focus since I'd seen her showing way too much skin.

"I said that I was thinking about moving to Africa to become a game warden. I asked you if I'd get eaten by a tiger."

"No game warden and no Africa," I told her. "Too dangerous."

And the only thing she might get eaten by was *me* if I couldn't douse my animalistic urges to make her mine.

"So what do you think I should do?" she asked.

I shrugged. "One thing at a time, Ruby. Get a license. Get your GED. And then you can decide."

The thought of her going anywhere made me crazy. I was pretty sure I'd be stalking her if she tried to leave.

"I know I'm going to be okay now, Jett. I can't take up residence forever in your guest bedroom," she said softly.

No. She couldn't. At least we agreed on one thing. She couldn't keep staying in the *guest* room. I needed her in *my* room...my bed.

The beast inside me that I couldn't seem to control didn't recognize the fact that she was safe.

I'd never see her as secure unless she belonged to me.

"Don't worry about that right now, Ruby. Let's just try to concentrate on getting your life the way it should have been."

"I don't think I can live here," she mused. "Seattle is too expensive."

Shit! The last thing I wanted was her planning a future *without me.* The feral animal inside me sat up and growled.

"You can live with me," I said insistently. Maybe *too* insistently. "I *want* you to stay with me."

Sure, she was going to have her own money, but I didn't care.

"I think you're a masochist," she said with a laugh.

Hell, I'm starting to think the same thing.

To have Ruby around and not want to nail her was impossible, but I was screwed because I didn't want her to go away, either.

No wonder I felt so damn ornery.

"But I'm going to have to think about the future soon," she said. "I'll eventually get my inheritance, and you've done so much for me already."

The money *had* changed everything, but I didn't regret giving Ruby her freedom by searching out the truth. Even though I wanted her to stay, I also wanted her to be happy.

"We'll work it out," I told her, knowing that I'd do whatever she really wanted in the end.

"I'll need your help," she ventured. "I'll have to figure out what a reasonable future looks like for me. Counseling has helped a lot, but I have so much to figure out."

I looked at her anxious expression, and every damn carnal thought I'd been having didn't mean a thing.

Ultimately, I'd be there for her because I cared too much about Ruby *not* to want her happiness. "I'll help you," I answered. "Everything will be okay."

I felt like a damn god when she smiled at me.

Maybe she needed a father figure.

Maybe she needed a friend.

Maybe she just needed somebody around who cared.

Whatever she needed, I'd turn myself inside out to give it to her. She'd been through too damn much already.

Chapter 16

Ruby

"I think that was the most incredible meal I've ever had," I said to Jett as we were on our way home from the restaurant.

I was feeling blissfully full, and completely relaxed from the wine I'd had with my seafood.

Jett had been acting a little off tonight, but maybe he was just tired. He'd been spending a lot of time in his office.

"I have a hard time believing that," Jett answered with amusement. "I've had better meals that you've cooked."

"But I don't generally cook seafood since I didn't grow up near water. Beef and chicken were a lot more common. It was a big treat for me to get fresh seafood. Thank you for taking me there," I told him.

I was getting better at accepting the things that Jett did for me, and just letting him know I appreciated it instead of constantly arguing about the money he spent on me.

Annette had done a good job of reminding me that Jett could well afford whatever he gave, and he gave it because he cared.

I was tired of taking all the joy out of anything Jett and I did by feeling guilty about the money, and being poor was just something

I had to deal with right now. I wasn't going to get my money over-night, and I'd eventually find a job or a career so I could return the favor.

"You're welcome," Jett finally said in a husky voice as the car pulled up to his building.

He got out and reached for my hand to help me out of the car while he traded a few insults with Pete. This time it was a lot more obvious that the two of them loved to antagonize each other.

We rode the elevator in a comfortable silence, and Jett didn't speak until we got back into the condo. "Do you want another glass of wine?" he asked as he took his suit jacket off and tossed it over one of the kitchen chairs.

I took off the borrowed coat I was wearing and hung it in the closet by the door. "I'm not sure I should," I confessed as I moved toward the kitchen. "I haven't had much alcohol in my life, and I'm already feeling the glasses I had with dinner."

He took the cork off a bottle he'd pulled from his wine cooler, poured me half a glass, and slid it across the counter. "Live a little," he said with a grin. "This is a really nice vintage."

I took a cautious sip of the white wine, and was rewarded by an explosion of different tastes as the liquid flowed over my taste buds. "You're right," I said as soon as I swallowed. "It's really good."

Jett usually opted for something a little stronger, so I was sur-prised when he poured himself a glass and left the kitchen to chill out on the couch.

I watched as he put his legs up. "Are you okay?" I asked, concerned that maybe he'd done way too much walking earlier, before dinner and after.

I sat in the recliner directly across from him.

"Yeah. I'm good. Why?"

"We did a lot of walking, and you're still supposed to be resting your knee as much as possible."

He raised a dark brow as he answered. "I'm not exactly ancient and decrepit, Ruby. Even though thirty-one might seem old to you. I just have a bum knee."

I rolled my eyes at him. "I know you're not old. But I did cause you to injure yourself. And I know what you should be doing."

Jett appeared to be doing better, but I was still worried.

"I'm being good now," he joked. "And you're not allowed to nag since you refused to marry me. But that's probably a good thing since you can't stand me touching you."

We were both quiet. I hadn't expected him to go there because he never had. But maybe it was a good thing that he did. I'd been wanting to clear the air with him since the incident had happened, but I hadn't been able to summon the courage. But now that I knew he thought I had completely rejected him, I was done hiding from anything painful or humiliating with Jett.

If I'd hurt him even a little, I wanted to clear things up. I knew that I was ready.

Our relationship had become way more important to me than my secrets.

"It wasn't *you* that night, Jett," I said as I set my empty wine glass on the side table.

"There wasn't anybody else in the room," he scoffed. "But it's not your fault that there's nothing there for you, Ruby. I sure wished that I could say the same, but my dick is still hard every moment that you're with me."

His words caused a flutter in my stomach, but I couldn't get distracted, no matter how much I wanted to explore the tantalizing revelation he'd just made.

"There *was* somebody else in the room. I was there," I said as I pushed my hair back from my face nervously.

He turned his head toward me sharply. "What does that mean? Ruby, I heard you say that you could see the scars. You were desperate to get away from me. Let's not bullshit each other anymore. Do I wish that you were as attracted to me as I am to you? Hell, yes. But I'm still going to be your friend."

I stood up, angry at myself because I hadn't immediately told him the truth after the incident occurred.

Jett was attracted to me. Although his words blew me away, I knew it was true. And I *had* hurt him over the whole incident.

"And what happened before that? Was I pushing you away? Or was I kissing you back?" I challenged.

He shrugged. "I guess you finally came to your senses."

"This. Is. Not. About. You." I emphasized every word. "When you grabbed my ass, I got lost in bad memories. I had flashbacks, and not about *your* body. It was about *mine*."

"Your body is perfect, Ruby," Jett rumbled.

"Oh, do you think so?" My voice was getting louder, and my anxiety higher, but it was way too late to hold anything back. I needed Jett to understand why I reacted the way I did. "I have a few scars of my own. Most of them are psychological, but a few are still visible."

I walked over to where he was sitting and slowly lifted my dress to my waist, turned, and lowered the black cotton bikinis I had on so he'd finally get what I was trying to tell him. I hadn't been able to find the words, and I thought a visual would make things clearer.

Jett suck in a loud breath, and then he was silent.

I knew he was seeing the remnants of the whippings I'd taken throughout my childhood and adolescence.

"So when you grabbed my ass, I *did* freak, but not because of you," I explained. "You can see the old marks, but the wounds on my soul are a lot worse. My uncle molested me, Jett. And every time he did it, he beat me because he said it was all my fault. I've started to understand that he wasn't really beating *me*; he was whipping his own demons. It started in grade school, and it just got worse. He seemed to have a thing about asses, and when he felt me up, it hurt, especially when I was younger."

I let my dress fall, and I sat back down in my recliner, my face still flushed with embarrassment.

I reminded myself that it was *his* shame and not *mine*, but I was still trying to accept that completely.

"Tell me everything," Jett growled.

I lowered my head as I picked up and played with the wine glass. I may not be able to look at Jett, but I was going to be completely honest with him. "I never told my parents. My uncle told me that my parents would lose everything if I told them. I wasn't really old enough to understand that it would take more than half ownership of the business to ruin them. All I knew back then was that I was terrified something would happen to my family. As I got older, I guess I was programmed to believe him."

"Jesus Christ!" Jett exploded. "How could that happen when your parents were around?"

"When they were alive, it only happened when he could get me alone with him, and I tried to never let that happen. But since my parents didn't know, and my uncle was our only close relative besides my grandmother, I ended up alone with him occasionally. Sometimes, he didn't have the opportunity for months. But it didn't matter because he *always* had control. I was *always* afraid of the next time."

"No kid should ever have to live like that," he rasped. "What happened after your parents died, Ruby?" he asked in a graveled voice.

I shuddered as I remembered the event that had forced me to leave. "He started going beyond just touching after my parents were gone. I finally *had* to leave because he tried to rape me, Jett. I got away, but I knew I could never go back."

I saw a tear drop onto my dress, and when I lifted my hand to my face, I realized it was *drenched* with tears. I'd thought I was all cried out from baring everything in counseling the last several weeks. Apparently, I was wrong.

"Did you talk to Annette about all this?" Jett asked.

"Not at first. But I eventually talked it all out with her. It's not an easy thing to share with anybody. You and Dr. Romain are the only ones who know."

I could see Jett move out of the corner of my eye, so I wasn't surprised when I heard his calming voice above me. "Look at me, Ruby," he requested in a persuasive tone.

I tossed my hair back and tilted my head to finally look at his face. His expression was a myriad of emotions, from concern to fury.

He held out his hand, and I took it without hesitation. He pulled me to my feet, his eyes never leaving my face.

"I want to touch you, but I won't if you don't want me to," he said in a steady tone.

I more than *wanted* it; I *craved* it.

I put my arms around his neck. "I've never *not* wanted you," I confessed. "Promise me that whatever happens, you'll know it's not about you. I have a lot of baggage that I'm carrying, and it's going to take time to figure it all out."

"I get that now," he said with regret. "I was just too damn involved in my own disappointment to see your fear for what it is. *That* won't happen again."

I lay my head on his shoulder as he ran a soothing hand up and down my back. "I missed this. I missed feeling you close to me so much," I whispered. "I feel so many things when I'm with you, and I want so much. But then my demons took over, and I pushed you away. And I wasn't sure how to talk about it until I figured things out with Annette."

"I should have given you that time," he said.

"You didn't know," I said simply.

"What do you feel now?" he asked.

"I ache, Jett. I want so much more, but I'm not sure how to ask for it. Everything was so confusing. I didn't think I wanted anybody to touch me, but I want...you. I don't know if you feel the same way."

"I do, baby. More than you'll ever know."

"Then I wasn't sure if you'd want me after I told you what happened. Even though I'm technically a virgin, I still felt...dirty."

"Don't, Ruby," he rasped harshly in my ear. "You're perfect. None of that was ever your fault."

"I think I might be starting to understand that I was just the object. I wasn't a *person* or *family* to my uncle. I was a *thing* that tempted his sick mind. That's why he beat me after it happened. He had to blame something, so he blamed me."

I could feel Jett rocking my body gently, apparently trying to comfort me.

"Never again, Ruby. Never again," he said, like it was an oath.

"I'm free, Jett. You helped get me get myself back again. I can't promise you that I'll never have a knee-jerk reaction, but I'm healing."

"You need time, sweetheart," he crooned.

"Then why do I want you so much? Why do I ache so badly it hurts?" I asked, allowing myself to trust Jett with my feelings. "I want to be close to you."

"I want that, too," he said in a voice hoarse with emotion. "Look at me again, sweetheart," he cajoled.

I lifted my eyes and turned my head.

"Keep your eyes on me, Ruby. Don't look away. If you get the least bit uncomfortable, you have to tell me."

I agreed with a jerky nod.

His soothing strokes down my back got longer and his hand finally moved over the top of my ass. My breath caught, but I kept my eyes on his, reminding myself that the touch was coming from somebody I trusted, somebody who would *never* hurt me.

I was seeing through the eyes of an adult woman, and all I could see was Jett.

He took things slow, so by the time he finally had my rear cupped in his gentle hold, I was completely comfortable.

"This is an ass that should have been worshiped once you were old enough to explore your sexuality," he told me in an anguished voice. "You're so fucking sweet, Ruby. Nobody should have ever done anything to you except love you. You know that now, right?"

I nodded. "Rationally I understand it, but I was programmed to believe otherwise. I always thought it was my fault, that I'd done something bad to deserve it. But since I started counseling and reading books by survivors, I know it's not true. I just have to retrain my brain, and it's not going to happen overnight."

I fell into his ferocious gaze, not even realizing when he'd pulled up my dress and laid his hands on my bare skin.

Truth was, I knew it was Jett, and my fear was slowly fading away completely.

I *wanted* him to touch me.

I *wanted* him to kiss me again like there was no other woman in the world who he wanted.

I *wanted*...everything.

"Will you help me?" I asked, unable to keep the longing from my voice.

"With whatever you need, baby," he vowed.

"I want you to help me explore my sexuality. I think I'm way behind. I hated my body so much that I didn't even masturbate. I don't even know what pleasure and orgasms feel like."

His eyes flamed with heat as he looked at me incredulously. "Ruby, I'm not sure that's—"

"Please," I interrupted. "I know you're not a virgin, and if I don't do this with you, I don't think I can do it with anybody else. I want to learn to live, Jett. I don't want to let my past define who I am anymore. I don't want to be a victim. I want to be a desirable woman."

His hands stroking over my bare ass was anything *but* unpleasant, and I could feel my body responding to him with a need I'd never known before.

His expression turned into a smirk. "I won't lie, Ruby. I like sex. I've *always* liked it. And I had no problem exploring my sexuality from the time I realized I had a dick, and that it felt good to play with it."

Jett was unabashedly blunt, but him talking about exploring his own sexuality as a kid actually helped.

"Then you can help me," I concluded.

"I'm not sure I can."

I never stopped to consider the fact that maybe Jett just didn't want to have sex with me. "You don't want me anymore," I stated sadly.

He shook his head. "I don't think I've ever wanted anyone more than I want you. But you're a virgin, Ruby."

"I understand. It's probably not very appealing if I can't please you."

"I don't give a shit about that," he grunted. "I care about whether I know how to pleasure a virgin. And if I'm the right guy to take your virginity away from you."

"I want it to be you," I argued softly. "And you can't take it if I'm already offering it to you."

He let out a short, guttural sound as he lowered his head to my shoulder and said, "Then God help me, because I'm going to be the man who does."

Chapter 17

Jett

I knew I was totally and completely fucked.

For me, once I'd made Ruby mine, there was going to be no going back.

I lifted my head, my body still tense as I sat back down on the couch and pulled Ruby's soft, feminine, and willing body onto my lap.

It wasn't going to happen *tonight,* and it may not happen *for weeks.* But eventually, Ruby Kent *was* going to be mine.

"I don't want to squash your leg," Ruby squealed as she made herself comfortable, trying to make sure she wasn't on top of my bum knee.

My leg didn't hurt nearly as much as my engorged, aching dick right now.

"You're fine. Keep still," I demanded. If she didn't stop grinding her beautiful ass against my hard-on, I was going to have a harder time being patient.

And Ruby was going to require all the finesse I had.

My first objective was just to make her comfortable with being touched and sharing her personal space with me.

After that, I'd have to play it by ear.

All I knew was I wanted her to trust me, and that wasn't going to happen by me bending her over the nearest object and fucking her until my gut-gnawing need for her was satiated.

I wished her uncle was still alive so I could make him die painfully for all that he'd done to hurt Ruby, but this wasn't about *me*. It was about *her*, and what Ruby needed now was somebody to trust, and somebody who cared about her.

And she had both of those things with me.

Just the thought of somebody hurting a hair on her head made me crazy, so I couldn't even think about what had been done to her as an innocent child.

She's so fucking beautiful!

If I wanted to be honest, I'd admit that I'd been screwed since the very first time I'd seen her, and it was about time I got totally real. And it wasn't just because her beautiful body had been on display. What had grabbed my balls and squeezed them until it was painful was the way Ruby had been able to keep her chin up, and was unwilling to let *anyone* see her emotions. She had been terrified, but she didn't give anybody the satisfaction of knowing just how scared she was.

I'd admired her courage since day one, and I still did. But now I also loved her intelligence, her humor, and just about every damn thing about her.

She could probably tell me to fuck off, and I'd love that, too.

"Are we going to have sex tonight?" she asked.

I loved her newfound candor, and my cock was beyond ready to have sex with her. But my brain definitely *wasn't*.

Putting my hand behind her head, I pulled her down to kiss the gorgeous lips that had been tempting me all damn night.

A tiny squeak of pleasure vibrated against my mouth, and all I could think about was making her crazy with need. I wanted to hear her moans as I drew her closer and closer to climax.

As I released her mouth, I said, "We're going to take this slow, Ruby. There's so much more to being pleasured than just a fuck."

She didn't have a clue how good an orgasm could feel, and I wanted to teach her every way she could get there.

"I've read books," she said with a sigh. "But it only explains the physiological things."

"You still don't touch yourself?" I asked.

"Only a few times while I've been with you. I feel like my body is waking up to sensations I've never had before. But I'm not quite sure what to do."

"No foreplay in high school? Not even first or second base?"

"I never even got into the stadium," she said unhappily. "I wasn't the pretty, cheerleader type, so most guys gave me a wide berth. And even if they hadn't, I wasn't allowed to date until I was sixteen, and that was the year my parents died. And honestly, I had no desire to get close to anybody male except my dad."

I started thinking about her uncle again, but I shut the thoughts down so I could put my attention where it needed to be—on her.

Ruby shifted off my lap, but plastered her body against mine and put her head on my shoulder.

"I guess I still don't understand how nobody noticed the fact that you were being abused. There had to be signs, Ruby."

"People see what they expect to see. Our home was outside of the city, in a smaller town. My uncle was an expert manipulator. For the most part, everybody liked him."

She was right. Abuse went undetected a lot. I'd made a point out of studying it since I'd met Ruby. I was pretty sure that Ruby had kept a low profile in school, and the only one who might have been able to save her had been her parents—had they known about it.

Unfortunately, it sounded like her uncle had struck terror in Ruby's heart about her family being broken up and harm coming to her parents if she told.

I wrapped my arms tightly around Ruby, glad that she had crossed *my path*, even if it had been traumatic for her. I didn't want to think about where she might be if she hadn't.

"You're safe now," I told her after I'd swallowed the huge lump in my throat.

She rubbed against me like a kitten. "I know."

Ruby had answered without hesitation, and it humbled me to know that she felt safe with me. She'd been through so damn much. I wasn't so sure I could be as trusting as she was if I'd lived her life.

"How much work do you have for me tomorrow?" she asked.

"Honestly?" I asked.

"Of course."

"Not much," I confessed. "Shirley helps me when I need it. I have a lot to do, but most of it is technical. I only offered you the job to get you here. I wanted to help you get on your feet and decide what you wanted to do with your life, but I knew you'd refuse to let me just help you out."

She looked up at me with a frown. "You lied to me?"

Dammit! I couldn't believe I actually felt guilty about bullshitting her so I could help her. "I stretched the truth. And I could actually use the help you've been giving me by cooking. I suck at it, and fast food gets old."

"I know I haven't exactly been reasonable, Jett. But it's hard for me to take anything from anybody. I want to make my own way."

"I get that," I answered. "But you have to learn that sometimes you have to take the help you need along the way to get where you want to be in life."

"You're right," she capitulated. "But be patient with me. I'm not used to anybody wanting to help me."

When I looked at Ruby, I saw a gentle soul who had been abused and hurt so badly that she wasn't quite sure who she was anymore. But in just the short time we'd been together, she'd changed. Ruby was rapidly righting the wrongs in her life. And I didn't want to fuck that up. "I shouldn't have lied to you," I confessed. "But I was pretty desperate."

"Don't," she said, putting her fingers over my lips. "You're a good man, Jett. I know you don't just lie for no reason. So you want me to cook. What else?"

I shrugged. "We'll make the rest up as we go along."

"I'd really like to get a driver's license, and I want to schedule my GED."

I nodded. "Those should both be a priority. What have you always wanted to be, Ruby? If you could do anything you wanted to do, what would it be?"

"I guess I've never really thought about it because I've always wanted to be a pastry chef."

"I think we have culinary schools here," I mused.

Ruby punched me lightly on the arm. "Of course you do. There are some good ones here."

"And I definitely recommend working for yourself," I told her with a grin. "Working for other people sucks."

She rolled her eyes. "Says the tech giant who has more money than he knows what to do with. I might have to start small."

I didn't tell her that I was more than willing to be her partner if she wanted her own place. Hell, I'd give her a bakery, but I knew she wouldn't accept that. "You can figure out your plan while you're going to school, if you decide that's what you want to do. You have time."

"I'm going to work, even if I decide to go to school," she said firmly.

"You're working for me," I reminded her.

"I need to start supporting myself, Jett," she said stubbornly. "And cooking for you is *not* working for you. I have to eat, too. And I need to find my own place once I get my inheritance."

"Don't go there, Ruby," I growled.

I understood the fact that she wanted to feel valuable by working and taking care of herself, but it was a hell of a lot more important for her to figure out what her goals were first.

"Okay. We'll talk about it later. We could have sex instead," she teased.

"Don't go *there*, either," I warned.

"Will you kiss me then?"

F. A. Scott

Every muscle in my body was tight as I looked at her sultry, hopeful expression.

There was no damn way I was going to say no.

Chapter 18

Ruby

I was getting bold.

But I was desperate.

I held my breath until Jett's mouth came down on mine, sending a spark to every cell in my body.

Jett didn't just *kiss* me. He *owned* everything he touched. I sank into his warmth, and opened to him because I wanted everything he was willing to give me.

He devoured me like a man who had been hungry for way too long, and I felt the same urgency as I wrapped my arms around his neck.

I needed him to give me *something* because my body was urging me to seek more.

Heat flowed between my thighs, and something inside me clenched, begging for something elusive I didn't understand.

"Jett," I gasped as he released my mouth and started nipping and licking at the sensitive skin of my neck.

I fell back on the couch as he moved next to me and over me with a powerful presence that made me even more desperate for him to make the painful need I was experiencing go away.

"I need…" I whimpered, my voice trailing off because I didn't know exactly what I had to have.

"I know what you need, sweetheart," he said in a husky voice beside my ear.

I shivered as his hand moved under my dress and up my thigh, making my skin burn with heat everywhere he touched.

I almost jumped out of my skin as his fingers moved my panties aside and met my wet sex.

"Look at me, Ruby," he demanded.

Not realizing I'd closed my eyes, I opened them and immediately met his steely gaze.

"Don't look away. I want you to remember who you're with and not the past."

Every touch, every word he spoke was so intense that I didn't think my mind was going *anywhere* else. It couldn't. I was mesmerized by Jett.

"Show me what I need," I pleaded.

"This," he rasped.

I moaned as I felt his strong fingers stroke over my clit.

"Oh, God," I whimpered.

"Don't close your eyes," he demanded.

Instinctively, I wanted to escape in the sensual world he was building, so it was hard to stay focused on his face.

His touch was gentle, but demanding. He explored me, and I let my legs fall apart, silently entreating for more.

My body was restless, searching for something just out of my reach as I lifted my hips and rubbed hard against his marauding fingers.

"I think I need you to fuck me," I said in a breathless voice.

"No, you don't," Jett answered in a graveled voice. "Do you trust me, Ruby?"

"Yes," I whimpered as I felt myself quivering with need. I had faith that Jett could take care of almost anything, including the fire he'd started inside me.

"Then close your eyes, remember that I'm right here, and let yourself feel everything. Don't think about anything else except pleasure."

My eyes slammed closed, thinking that if what he was doing was less intense, maybe my body would stop aching.

It didn't.

I fell into a darkness that only allowed me to feel the madness even more.

His strokes grew bolder and harder, giving me some of the rougher pressure I instinctively knew I needed.

"Please," I cried out.

"Relax," he crooned. "Just feel."

"I feel too much," I gasped out.

"Because it's new. It's not too much. You're wet and you're so ready to come."

I felt him penetrate me with one of his fingers, and I mewled, my head starting to thrash with frustration.

"You're so tight, sweetheart," he said gently.

I let out a loud moan, and lifted my hips again urgently.

I wasn't too sure how long I could handle the pleasure and torment of what he was doing to me.

He retreated and completely focused on the tiny bundle of nerves that were throbbing for attention.

Harder.

Faster.

And so mind-blowing that I felt the tight ball in my belly start to unfurl and shoot straight between my thighs, intensifying an ache that was almost unbearable.

"Yes. Yes, please," I urged him on mindlessly.

My body started to tremor and I experienced nothing but pleasure waving over my entire body as I helplessly tried to hold onto my sanity.

"Jett!" I screamed as I reached some kind of pinnacle.

His mouth slammed over mine as though he wanted to swallow my gratification. I kissed him roughly as my body started to wind down, never wanting to let my beautiful man go.

I was panting as he finally moved his hand from my sex.

I watched as he put his fingers into his mouth one by one and sucked my juices from the digits.

"Someday, I'm going to taste your pussy, and lick every sweet drop," he said gruffly as he looked into my eyes.

I shivered, and my body went taut all over again. Yeah, I knew about oral sex. I wasn't uneducated about the human body—not in theory. But after what had happened, I couldn't imagine how intense that experience would be.

My mouth was suddenly dry. I licked my lips before I asked, "Will I get to do that to you?"

His eyes grew fierce as he answered, "Maybe. Some women don't like to do that."

"I think I'd love it," I answered eagerly, wondering what it would be like to pleasure Jett until he lost control.

He smirked at me as he made us comfortable lying close and face-to-face, his arm tightly around my waist. "Baby, there aren't many guys who would turn it down."

"Is it better than having sex?" I asked curiously. Now that I had somebody who had a plethora of knowledge, and wasn't shy about talking about sex, I wanted to know everything.

He shook his head slightly. "Not better. Just different."

"I want to do everything with you," I confessed.

He stroked my hair back from my face as he said, "We need to take this slow, Ruby. It's not easy because I want you so bad that my balls are constantly blue, but I need to get this right. Did what we did scare you?"

"I think it's a knee-jerk reaction to be alarmed for a second," I explained. "But I think I want to be with you so much that it goes away before I ever really acknowledge it. I want to know what I've been missing, and what I never got a chance to figure out because of my past. And somehow I know I can only do that with you."

He ran a hand through his hair in what appeared to be frustration. "Nothing needs to happen fast, Ruby. And I need you to tell me if something feels wrong."

I smiled at him mischievously. "What you did felt pretty damn right to me. My only regret is that you didn't get anything out of it. It doesn't seem fair."

I wanted to please Jett, too. I didn't want my sexual introduction to be entirely one-sided, and I knew how it felt to need.

"It will happen eventually," he promised. "And don't ever think that I don't get anything out of hearing you scream my name while you come. It gives me satisfaction, and it's pretty damn good for my ego."

"I'm sure you already knew that you were good in the sex department," I said drily.

"I do," he agreed arrogantly. "But it's been awhile for me, Ruby. I haven't been with anyone since the accident."

I frowned at him. "Why?"

"Lisette's rejection destroyed my confidence, I guess. I didn't want to get naked because of my scars. And I'm not as athletic as I used to be because of my leg."

My heart ached, and once again, I really wanted to hurt Lisette. "I wish I could bitch-slap her," I said angrily. "Honestly, Jett, I understand that you lost some of your confidence, but you're still drop-dead gorgeous, ripped like a male model, and you're in incredible physical shape except for your leg. And I still want to take a bite of your ass every time I see you. Who cares about a few scars when you have so much to offer any woman? You're special. You said that finding pleasure is much more than just a fuck. I don't think many men really think that way."

Jett chuckled and kissed me on the forehead. "You are good for my ego, Cinderella," he said, his voice overflowing with humor.

"You should *already have* a healthy ego about *everything*," I insisted. "You have everything a woman could ever want, and I'm not talking about all the money you have. That's just a bonus."

"Most women don't think like you do, either," Jett said in a more serious tone. "Not in my world."

"Then you need to find *another world*, because I think yours is full of silly, superficial bimbos," I told him emphatically.

I couldn't see how any woman could look at Jett and not want him.

He grinned at me. "I guess there are a few good ones, like Dani and Harper. But they never really lived in our world. Harper made a career out of building homeless shelters all over the country, giving away her skills as an architect, and you know what Dani is like."

"Did you love Lisette?" I asked, knowing I'd asked him about that before, but hoping I might get a more thorough answer this time.

"I thought I did," he explained thoughtfully. "But when I look back on our relationship, she pretty much orchestrated everything. And I just accepted it. I went to engagements and events that she thought were important, and I can see now how we really didn't spend any time together alone. I don't think we ever truly got to know each other. I didn't see anybody else, and when she hinted that it was time to get married, I just went along with it. I was so busy all the time between volunteering for PRO, and working my part of the business to keep it growing. I guess I never questioned my relationship because I'd gotten used to Lisette. Now, I wonder how I never noticed that she'd never even said that she loved me."

My heart squeezed painfully in my chest. "I know she hurt you, but you're so much better off without her," I said softly as I stroked his jawline. "You can rebuild your ego."

"I think you're doing that for me, Cinderella," he said with a laugh.

"And I'll keep on doing it until you think the same way as I do about yourself."

He raised a brow. "I don't think I'm ever going to want to take a bite out of my own ass."

A laugh escaped from my lips before I replied, "But you'll know that you deserve the best."

"I wish you knew that, too," he retorted. "Then maybe you wouldn't argue about taking things that you need right now."

"I'm working on it," I said. "I'm just so used to struggling alone. It's hard for me, Jett. I went for a very long time not feeling like I deserved anything."

"But you're technically mine for now," he said thoughtfully. "If we were really a couple, would it be so difficult?"

If Jett was mine, I'd feel like the luckiest woman in the world. "But we aren't, really."

"We could be," Jett suggested. "And I'd feel a whole lot better about being your sexual education teacher if we were trying to build a relationship. I care about you, Ruby. I want to be your guy. All you have to do is say *yes*. I have no idea where it will all go, but we have more than some couples do. We're attracted to each other, and we're friends."

I looked at the sincerity in his gorgeous eyes. "You can't possibly mean that."

"I've never meant something more," he argued. "I value our friendship, but I think both of us want more. Let's figure out how much more together."

Never in a million years would I have thought that Jett would want to try to have a real relationship with *me*. "I want to be your friend. But I want to be close to you, too," I said honestly.

"Then be mine," he said persuasively. "If we're together, then it would make sense that I would do everything I could to help you and vice versa. That's what couples do, right?"

He'd *been* part of a couple, and I found it sad that he had to ask that question.

"What would you get out of it?" I asked in a tremulous voice.

"That's easy," he answered swiftly. "I'd get *you*."

"A homeless woman who has no future and not even a high school education?" I said sadly.

"Don't say that," he said angrily. "I'd get the bravest, most beautiful, intelligent, and talented woman I've ever met. Don't put yourself down because of your circumstances, Ruby. That's not who you are.

Being homeless wasn't your fault. If anything, I admire your courage. You've kept fighting because nobody was there for you. But I'm here now. And I'm not going anywhere."

It was at that exact moment that I realized that I was totally, completely, and irrevocably in love with Jett Lawson. Maybe I'd already been falling for him, but I wasn't *falling* anymore. I'd landed with a *thud*, and gotten slammed over the head with the knowledge that he'd always be the man I wanted.

And the thought terrified me.

"Whatever is going through that beautiful head of yours right now, get rid of it. You look scared," Jett grumbled.

"I am," I confessed. "I want to say *yes* more than I've ever wanted anything, but you're way out of my league."

"Yeah, well, I think you're way out of mine, too. But I'm still asking."

"Is the relationship going to be real?" I asked, still not understanding why he actually wanted me. I was already more than willing to have sex with him.

"As real as it gets," he answered firmly. "Say yes, Ruby. What do we have to lose?"

My heart. I could lose my heart.

I took a deep breath and remembered what I'd learned so far in therapy.

My reality isn't what other people think or see. It's distorted because of my background.

While I was struggling *not* to see myself as a complete loser who didn't deserve anything good to happen to her, Jett obviously saw me way differently.

And God, I wanted to be the woman he wanted to see every single day.

Happiness was within my grasp. All I had to do was reach out and grab it.

Problem was, I didn't want to lose it again. I'd be devastated.

He's worth it.

I sighed as I looked at the face of the man who had changed my life.

I might be afraid, but if I didn't try to make our relationship real, I knew I'd always regret it.

"Yes," I finally said in a mesmerized tone.

"You won't be sorry," Jett said fiercely. "I'll do everything in my power to make sure you never wish you hadn't taken me on. And I'll be happy that you can't argue about me giving you the things you need."

"I don't think that was part of the deal," I said hurriedly.

He gently pushed a stray lock of hair from my face as he answered, "Ruby, if you're mine, you share my life. It's going to be give-and-take. It's not in me to have a woman and not give her everything I can to make her life easier."

I sighed. "I know," I conceded. "But it's not really fair because I don't have a lot to give except myself. Not right now."

Eventually, I'd have my inheritance, but I didn't have a penny of my own yet.

"That's all I want," he answered. "I think in a good relationship, things go back and forth. I can guarantee that there are going to be times when I'll need you more than you need me in the future, and you'll have your chance to be there for me. But right now, let's just get this new life moving."

It was hard for me to imagine a time when Jett wasn't the strong one in our relationship, but I was going to do everything I could to make his words a reality. I was going to fight for my success, and give back all that he had given me emotionally.

I gave him a small smile. "I think I'm ready."

He grinned. "I know I am," he declared right before he sealed the deal with a toe-curling kiss that wiped all negative thoughts from my brain for the rest of the night.

Chapter 19

Ruby

"Oh, my God, Ruby. These are incredible," my new friend, Lia, claimed as she took a bite of my pastry.

The last week had been the happiest and most exciting of my life. After a few days of study and tutoring from Pete, I'd taken my driver's test and passed, so I now had a valid driver's license.

I had just spent a grueling day of testing for my GED, and I was hoping I'd done well enough to start taking some college courses.

And I'd met two new friends, the owners of Indulgent Brews, Lia and Zeke. I'd stopped by the coffee place across the street from Jett's condo the day after Jett and I had started the new chapter in our relationship, and struck up a conversation with Lia as I was getting a latte. Although the shop was well-known for their coffee, they'd recently tried adding pastries and it had been an epic fail, according to Lia. I told her I could try to help her find something better, and I'd brought her some of my own pastries to try to get a feel for what she liked.

Lia had just demolished the frosted orange and poppy seed buns, and was starting on the chocolate caramel brownies.

I'd tried to bring her a few things I thought would pair well with coffee, and do well in her store.

What she was carrying now was bite-sized pastries that didn't really hold all that well throughout the day. And in my opinion, they just weren't big enough. When I had coffee, I wanted a pastry to hold me over until my next meal. I wanted something more satisfying than tiny bites.

"I need these," Lia groaned as she licked her fingers and then went to wash her hands after totally killing off the large brownie.

"I think I can help you find the right vendor," I said. I might not know all of the bakeries in Seattle, but I could browse through them until I found the right products.

She tossed her paper towel in the trash and turned to me as she said, "I'm looking at her. I need *your* pastries."

Lia was a pretty, petite, and curvy blonde who loved to chat with customers. Normally, I wasn't very social because I hadn't had much of a social life, but Lia made everybody feel comfortable when she was around.

As a teenager, I'd loved talking to vendors and helping my mom get the products she needed.

"I'm not really a professional," I said in a rush.

"Your talent says otherwise," she said as she stared steadily at me. "I ate a lot of pastries when I was looking for the right ones, and none of them were *this good*."

"I had a good teacher," I told her. "But I haven't gone to pastry school."

"There's something to be said for natural talent and experience," she said. "Let's make a deal," she said persuasively.

"Making deals without me?" a male voice said from the door of the small kitchen and storage area.

"Zeke!" Lia squealed. "I found our pastries."

I watched as Lia's partner and friend entered the serving area. Zeke was incredibly attractive in a dark suit and tie that made his hair look lighter than its usual light brown.

It was hard to believe that Zeke and Lia weren't a couple. They squabbled and joked like they'd been together forever. But Lia was getting married to somebody else, so there was nothing romantic happening, even though I noticed that Zeke looked at Lia like he adored her.

He strolled over and peeked into the box I'd brought. "Two spots are empty," he observed as he took out a cinnamon roll, the only thing left in the box.

"You're lucky I don't care for cinnamon," she told him. "Or that one would be gone, too."

Zeke took a huge bite and swallowed before he said, "I'm on board. Where can we get these?"

"Ruby made them. I'm trying to talk her into making our pastries for us."

"These are really good, Ruby. I hope you agree," Zeke said with a charming smile.

"I was just telling Lia that I'm not a professional."

"All that matters is the quality of the product that comes out of the oven," Zeke said as he finished off the cinnamon roll. "And this is perfect."

"They were *all* perfect," Lia added.

"Knowing you, Ruby's not leaving until she agrees," Zeke teased his partner.

"You know it," Lia told him.

"I can't stay," Zeke said as he headed for the kitchen. "I just came by to pick up my phone. I left it here this morning."

I saw disappointment in Lia's expression. She was obviously fond of her business partner. But Zeke had a career, and Lia had told me that he was the silent partner who had put up the capital while she ran the store.

But for a silent partner, Zeke seemed to be in the shop *a lot.*

"Nice seeing you, Ruby," Zeke called. "Keep making the cinnamon rolls for me."

I smiled as he disappeared through the back door. He seemed like such a nice guy.

"He's such a good partner," Lia said wistfully.

"He is," I agreed. "I'm surprised you're not a couple. What's your fiancé like?"

"Oh, Stuart is *nothing* like Zeke," she said as she leaned back against the counter. "Stuart is so organized. He never would have lost his phone. He's perfect in every way."

Honestly, I think I preferred somebody who was *human*, but Lia obviously appreciated her fiancé's perfection. "Are they friends? Zeke and Stuart?"

"Oh, God, no. Stuart says Zeke is brash and annoying, but he doesn't understand Zeke. Stuart doesn't really have a sense of humor, and Zeke loves to joke."

"I think you like that, too," I commented.

"Only with Zeke," she said hesitantly.

Lia was so upbeat that it was hard to believe that she didn't like to trade amusing things with the man she loved, but I didn't really know her well enough to say anything else.

"So about this pastry deal…" Lia said. "Zeke was right. I'm going to have to persuade you to give us those pastries."

She started to talk, naming a price that seemed like a small fortune to me.

"Let me think about it," I told her when she was done laying out her plan. "I'd really like to do it, but I want to talk to Jett about it first."

"What are you talking to me about?" Jett's voice sounded from the entrance. "Whatever you want, you know it's always going to be a *yes*."

I sighed as I turned around and saw Jett near the door. He was dressed in a pair of black jeans and a green button-down shirt that made his eyes look even sexier than they were already.

"Is everything okay?" I asked, wondering why he'd come to find me.

"It's good now. I was just getting a little worried. It's after seven."

I'd told Jett that I'd be stopping here, but that I'd be home before six. "I'm sorry. Time got away from me."

"Actually," Lia chimed in. "I was holding her hostage until she agreed to make her pastries for us. They're incredible."

Jett stopped in front of me and kissed me on the forehead. "I couldn't agree more. And did you get her to agree?"

"Not yet. But I'm working on it," Lia replied.

"She doesn't need my approval," Jett told Lia. "So you'll just have to convince *her.*"

Lia beamed at him as she folded her arms. "A trial run?" she suggested. "If everything goes well, then we can make the deal."

I nodded. "Let's do it."

We decided to make the following week the trial, and I wasn't about to argue about her price.

Jett waited patiently without speaking until we'd hammered out the details.

"I'm proud of you," he said as we left the shop. People began pouring in as we were leaving, obviously the after-work crowd that Lia had warned me about earlier.

"For what?" I asked as I took his hand.

I still wasn't used to Jett's frequent compliments, but I was learning not to brush them off like I used to.

Counseling was assisting me to navigate through the real world, and helping me understand that my own negative thoughts and self-perception were sabotaging me. I was trying to do everything I could to change that.

"You don't have any business experience, yet you've managed to get a contract with one of the most popular coffee shops in the city," he explained.

"It was kind of a happy accident," I replied.

"Don't brush this off, Ruby," Jett said sternly. "This was all you. You gave without expecting anything back. You were just trying to help Lia. But your pastries are so amazing that they sell themselves. That's your work, your special skill. You should be proud of yourself."

"I'm nervous," I confessed as we waited for the light to cross the street.

"Understandable. But you don't need to be. You make incredible things that everybody is going to want."

"I'll have to use your kitchen," I warned him. "And I'll need some equipment."

"Since I don't use the kitchen, it's all yours," he teased. "And you can either dip into your savings, or I'll get all the equipment you want. In return, you can make extras of everything for me. I think I'm getting the good end of the deal."

I smiled at him. I loved the way he always tried to make it seem like he was the lucky one. "I accept that deal," I said with laughter in my voice.

The light turned and we started to walk across the street.

"How was the test?" he asked as we made it to the other side.

"I think I did good. It didn't seem that bad. It was just a really long day."

"How long for the results?"

"They said that they'd probably be entered by the end of the day. I'll have to check the GED site."

"We'll check together when we get up to the condo, but I want you to come with me first," he said mysteriously as we stepped into the elevator and he keyed in access for the underground parking.

"Where are we going?" I asked, willing to let him take me wherever he wanted to go.

"You'll see," he said with a devilish grin.

When we stepped into the parking garage, Jett led me forward and then stopped in front of a small SUV that looked brand-new. I admired the gorgeous BMW that was a deep red color that was almost burgundy, and had what looked like a luxurious beige leather interior.

Jett reached into his pocket and handed me a small black object.

I took it, but I was confused. "What is this?"

"The keys for your new vehicle. Happy birthday, sweetheart."

I looked at the controller in my hand, and then at the beautiful BMW in front of us.

And my brain finally connected the dots.

"Mine?" I squeaked.

"All yours. I didn't want to go expensive because I knew you wouldn't like that. So I compromised. The X3 has a great safety rating."

I opened my mouth but nothing came out, so I ended up flapping my lips like a fish out of water.

"Do you like it?" Jett asked.

I put my hand gingerly on the hood and stroked the beautiful vehicle. "It's too much," I finally said between my bouts of hyperventilation. "Oh, my God. It's a BMW."

"It's not that expensive, Ruby. And I doubt you're going to like driving my expensive Bugatti or the Escalade I have for going to the mountains. And I don't think Pete is going to part with the sedan again after you used it for your driver's test."

I knew he was probably right. Pete had looked like a nervous wreck when he'd taken me to get my license, and had to part with his sedan while I used it to perform the required driving part of the exam.

I took some deep breaths to normalize my breathing and help my heart to slow down. "It's so beautiful," I said as I slowly made my way to the door and fumbled with the remote to open it.

"It's safe," Jett told me. "And reliable."

I finally unlocked the driver's door and slid inside.

The car smelled like leather and luxury, something that was so far beyond anything I knew that it was almost intoxicating.

I petted the smooth leather, marveling over every feature in the car.

"If you don't like it, I'll get you something else," Jett said softly from the open door. "I should have asked you, but I wanted to surprise you for your birthday."

I hadn't even *remembered* it *was* my birthday. But it touched me that Jett had known, and had obviously planned for it.

I clambered out of the vehicle and threw myself into his arms. "It's beautiful," I said with a sob. "I love the red. I love the size. I love everything about it."

"Then why are you crying?" he asked as he tightened his arms around me.

"I guess I was just...shocked."

He stroked my hair as he explained, "You're going to need a vehicle, and this is actually a compromise for me. It's a reasonably priced vehicle."

"A reasonably priced *luxury* vehicle," I corrected, not knowing whether I wanted to laugh or cry.

"I'm a guy, Ruby, and I want to know my woman is safe. Don't cut off my balls over a vehicle," he teased.

I started to laugh against his shoulder.

He'd won.

There was no way I was going to cut his balls off. I wanted them for myself too much.

Jett and I had started sleeping together, but as of yet, he hadn't gone beyond satisfying me with his touch. Although I coveted that intimate time with him, I wanted so much more.

"Thank you," I murmured. "I haven't really had a birthday since my parents died."

"There will never be another one that isn't a special day from now on," he vowed.

I hugged him tight. There wasn't a single day since I met Jett that *didn't* feel like a very special day. He made everyday things important in their own way.

"Let the party begin upstairs," he said lightly.

He'd obviously been waiting for me because it was my birthday, and he'd planned a celebration.

I swiped away the tears as I moved back and gave my beautiful transportation one more glance.

He pulled me back toward the elevator, and my soul felt lighter than it ever had before.

I knew it wasn't about *the gift*. It was all about the fact that Jett had actually made it his business to find out and *remember* my birthday.

I was starting to really feel like I was part of a couple.

And it felt pretty damn good.

Chapter 20

Ruby

"Oh, my God. Oh, my God." I put my hand over my mouth, still unable to believe what I was seeing on my laptop.

"Baby, what's wrong?" Jett asked from across the table.

We'd just finished a five-star dinner in the dining room of the condo that had been served to us one delicious course at a time.

The only thing left was the beautiful cake in the middle of the table after Jett had dismissed the dinner staff.

But before I cut the cake, I'd wanted to quickly see if I'd passed my GED exam.

"Jett, I think I passed," I said as I laughed like an idiot because I was so relieved to see that I'd passed in all areas of the test.

"I never doubted it, baby," he answered as he reached across the table and snagged my laptop.

After a moment, I settled down and looked at his pensive expression as he studied the results.

"What?" I said, alarmed. "Did I miss something? I passed, right?"

"Oh, you passed," he answered. "Ruby, you got a perfect score. You aced every single test. It's says you're college ready with credit, which means you might be able to get college credit because of your high scores if you want to go that route. How did you do this? Did you study?"

I shrugged. "I took some sample tests, but I didn't really study hard. I was always a good student. And I guess all my library time paid off."

"I think you're gifted," he answered. "I knew you were intelligent, but I didn't realize just how smart you really are."

I made a face at him. "I'm not, really. I just pick things up quickly."

He gave me a skeptical look. "Like math, science, art, and language?"

"I guess." I really hated to think about all the opportunities I'd missed. "I was in a lot of honors classes in school, so I was studying a lot of college material before I had to run away."

"Then you obviously had dreams, Ruby. Things you wanted to do with your life."

"I had a lot of *dreams*," I answered. "But I knew my *opportunities* weren't going to be there once my mom and dad died. I was applying for scholarships before they were killed, but my uncle insisted that I wasn't going to college because there was too much evil out there in the world. I guess he never really understood that the person I was the most afraid of was him."

"What did you want to do?" he asked.

"I was young, so I wanted to conquer the world, have cafes with the best pastries in every major city."

"Is that still what you want?"

I shook my head. "I don't think so. Being homeless…changed me. It helped me see a world that I'd never been in before. Homeless people talk to each other sometimes because we don't have anybody else. Granted, there are some people who are mentally ill and can't take care of themselves, but there are plenty of people on the streets just like me. Everybody has a story, and all of them are important. So many are just victims of circumstances in one way or another."

"I know," Jett responded. "My sister, Harper, says it makes her crazy. That's why she devoted her time to building places for them to go."

I shot him a small smile. "That's rare. A lot of people learn to ignore them."

"So what would you do now if you could do anything you wanted?"

"I'd like to be a pastry chef. I loved it, and it's something that was passed down from my mom. I know I need business classes, and maybe some higher culinary education, but I want to chase that dream now. And I'd like to do what I can as a volunteer for the homeless."

"Do you have a plan for how you'd help?" Jett asked.

I thought for a minute before I answered, "I'd love to run some shelters, but do more than just give them a place to sleep and eat. They need a hand up to get back into the working world and regain a sense of pride. I think that's one of the things we lose first, and it's hard to get that back again."

"I can find you the funding to develop a program," he suggested. "I'd be a solid donor, and I know a lot of business people who would support the cause. You'd earn a good salary for being the administrator if you want to do it full-time."

"I might end up turning down the salary," I teased. "I have a boyfriend who's filthy rich."

"Now you're getting the idea," he joked. "Use me."

I laughed because I knew he was teasing. It didn't surprise me a bit that Jett would donate. But I wasn't sure I was ready to start a commitment like that. "I'd need some time," I explained. "I don't have the business experience, and I'd need some help."

"Whenever you're ready, I'll be here. Homelessness is an area where I'd like to help out as much as possible."

"I noticed," I told him. "You've already done a lot of your own work on the side."

He shrugged. "I helped a few people. That's not nearly enough."

"If everybody who could afford it did what you did, we wouldn't have to worry about the homeless. Don't discount the things you do to help people who are in a bad place. It's pretty extraordinary."

"*You're* pretty extraordinary, Ruby Kent," he said in a husky tone.

My heart ached as I stared back at him, wondering what I'd ever done in my life to deserve a guy like Jett. "This has been the best birthday ever," I told him honestly.

I was kind of sad that I couldn't plan a birthday party for Jett in the near future, but his birthday had passed right before we'd met.

"It *will be* as soon as you cut that cake," he replied with a cheeky grin.

I hopped up to get some plates and a cake knife. "What kind is it?" I asked.

It was obviously chocolate because it was frosted with chocolate icing, but there was a light glaze over the top that I couldn't identify.

"Salted caramel chocolate cake," he announced. "I told the baker that you were a pastry snob, so it better be good."

"You didn't really say that," I told him confidently, knowing Jett was too nice to threaten a baker.

"Okay, I *didn't*," he acknowledged. "But I *did* tell her you were a pastry snob and asked which cake she recommended."

I really couldn't scold him for that. I was, in fact, a pastry snob. Not because I wanted to be, but because I couldn't help myself. My mom had made the best desserts in the state of Ohio, and I'd had the best when I was a kid.

I set the plates down, and cut the cake.

I almost salivated as I saw the caramel filling in the middle, and I could already tell it was moist.

"Looks good," I said as I handed Jett a large piece, and then cut myself a smaller one. "I'm actually still full from dinner."

"There's always room for dessert, sweetheart," he answered as he took the cake eagerly.

I sat down and savored my first bite. I still hadn't gotten to the point where I didn't appreciate having amazing food, or *any* food for that matter. I might have grown up on good food, but I'd been pretty damn hungry for the last six years or so.

"It's good," I said as I swallowed my first bite.

"High praise coming from you," he said playfully.

I made a face at him and continued to eat my cake.

He finished his and sat back in his chair. "So what's your plan for Lia's shop?"

"She needs something a lot different than she has, and that goes well with coffee. Like chocolate croissants, sweet buns, and maybe some incredible brownies. I'll sit down later and plan out what I'm making every day next week."

"Nobody has sweeter buns than you," he said in a cheerful voice.

I rolled my eyes. "Tell me you didn't just go there."

He shrugged. "I did. I couldn't help myself."

"It's going to feel good to finally be earning money."

"That could be a lucrative gig," he agreed.

"It's nothing compared to your net worth, but I'll take it."

"No offense, sweetheart, but there are very few people in the world who have my net worth. I'm not saying that to be arrogant. It's just a fact."

I knew he wasn't being conceited. No matter how many skills or how much education I got, my income would never be even a tiny fraction of his. "I'm not making comparisons anymore, and I'm not intimidated by your money. I let you give me a car, for God's sake. I think I'm doing pretty well with accepting that I'm with a very rich guy."

"I'm not downplaying your accomplishment, Ruby. I never would. Going out and snagging a gig with Lia's shop is huge. I know every eatery in the city will be fighting over you pretty soon."

"Do you think so?" I asked hesitantly.

He nodded. "I know so."

I basked in his praise for a moment, refusing to blow it off like I used to do.

I was smart.

I was ambitious.

I made tasty pastry.

And I was determined to make a difference in the world in my own way.

That was really all that I wanted.

"Thanks," I finally acknowledged quietly. "Thank you for always being there to encourage me. It means a lot."

Jett never acted like his career was more important than what I was doing, or that my interests or ambitions were ever inferior to his. He treated me like an equal, even though he was one of the most important and influential men in the world.

"If I didn't support you, it would make me a jerk," he considered. "And I'd hate being an asshole."

I laughed. "You're not. I wouldn't be with a jerk, no matter how much money he had."

He shot me a heart-stopping grin. "Besides, I might be slightly intimidated by your intelligence now. You might have a higher IQ than I do."

"No, you're not intimidated. You already know you're brilliant. The best hacker in the world, remember?"

Jett amazed me when he was in his "zone" on the computer. His fingers flew over the keys so fast that they were practically a blur. And he'd stop for a minute, and then move on, only to stop one more time and evaluate the screen before he seemed to get another idea and forged ahead. I'd watch him do that for hours sometimes, and he never seemed to get impatient or weary with what he was doing. It was obvious that he loved a challenge. And it didn't appear that he couldn't conquer every one of them.

"Are you still okay with going to Marcus's wedding with me?"

"Of course. When is it?"

"Two weeks," he said.

"I'm looking forward to it. I still want to thank Dani for what she did for me." I was silent for a moment before I said, "I really should get some clothes. But I'm not sure how to dress for the wedding of two billionaires."

The Colters and the Lawsons were both powerful families, and the wealth that would be amassed between them was almost unfathomable.

"Honestly, Dani isn't really that into clothes. She never has been. I'll admit that Marcus can be a little uptight, but only on the surface.

They're good people. They aren't going to care what you wear. They'll both just be glad you came. It's going to be a fairly small service in Rocky Springs, with the reception at the resort that Marcus's mom owns there."

"Are you in the wedding party?" I asked.

He grinned. "Best man. Marcus didn't want to have to choose between all his brothers."

"So I'll get to see that gorgeous ass in a tuxedo?" I teased.

"It's all yours, sweetheart," he said suggestively as he loaded our plates into the dishwasher and put the cake in the fridge.

"I wish," I mumbled.

"What did you say?"

"Nothing," I answered.

"I'm going to go hit the shower," he said as he moved toward the elevator.

Can I come with you?

I knew that Jett wanted to move slow, but my body was pleading with him to pick up the pace.

Was he waiting for me to make that move? Or did he just want to make sure I was ready before he took things any further?

I sighed as I gathered up my laptop and followed him upstairs.

Maybe it was beyond time for me to figure it out.

Chapter 21

Jett

I stripped and turned the shower on.

Every single day, I needed to get myself off to stop myself from starting something with Ruby that she might not want to finish.

I *had* to get some kind of relief. And every goddamn day, visions of Ruby and the way she'd looked and sounded during her first orgasm and every orgasm after that fucking haunted me.

I stepped into the shower and leaned back against the tile. "Fuck!" I cursed. *How much longer was I going to be able to handle the nearly combustible sexual tension that flared between us?*

Ruby was the one good thing that had ever happened to me as an adult other than the fact that I was incredibly successful because Lawson had catapulted into a tech giant, which didn't seem nearly as monumental as the woman who had given me her trust.

Ruby had permeated my damn soul, and there was nothing I could do to stop it. Her essence had become a part of me I couldn't live without.

I craved her like an addict craved drugs, and it was pretty much torture to look at her and not make her completely mine. Primal instinct battered at me to claim her in every way possible, but because of her past, I wanted to be careful not to scare her off.

But it's not her fault that I'm a horny bastard!

I'd already admitted to myself that maybe my hesitation wasn't *completely* about her. She practically pleaded with me to fuck her every night, an event that always ripped my heart out. She was ready. But maybe I…wasn't.

It was about me now.

I was too damn scared that I was going to end up losing her somehow.

And that was completely unacceptable.

Okay, maybe she *had* seen the scars on my upper body, and she'd accepted them. But my leg was a mangled mess. And I was pretty sure the whole *naked* package was pretty ugly.

Hell, I'd seen Ruby growing and changing while she was in counseling. She was finding her own way, and standing on her own two feet. Eventually, she'd receive the insurance money her parents had left for her. *Was I fucking afraid she'd eventually leave me?*

I clenched my fists, knowing *that* was exactly what I feared. But I was going to have to move past my own issues to keep Ruby. If I didn't, I'd *definitely* lose her.

She needed to become independent, and I wanted that for her.

So I'd eventually have to find out if she was willing to accept me with all my deformities.

Or not.

Problem was, the stakes were way too high for me this time.

She's not Lisette!

I knew she wasn't like my ex, and maybe that was part of the problem.

Losing Lisette had been a blessing.

Watching Ruby walk away would completely destroy me.

The stakes were too damn high for me to take a risk.

"Jett?" I heard Ruby's hesitant voice from outside the glass door of the shower.

As it started to open, a gut reaction made me spring into action.

I slammed the partially open door in her face as I bellowed harshly, "Get the fuck out! Leave! I don't want you here, Ruby!"

Even with the shower running, I could hear her audible gasp of dismay. "I'm sorry," she said tearfully. "I'm so sorry."

I could see her form move toward the bathroom door, and she was fumbling to get out.

"Goddammit!" I cursed.

I'd let my own insecurities hurt the woman who didn't deserve it.

Her loud sob gutted me, and the only thing that mattered was making sure Ruby was okay.

I was being an asshole, and I knew it.

I slammed my way through the glass door and slapped my hand on the door as she finally got it open to leave, preventing her from escaping.

"Don't," I growled as I pinned her body face first against the closed door. "Don't cry."

After I'd lived through sharing her sorrow at the cemetery, I never wanted to see Ruby hurt that way again.

The meeting of our bodies skin-to-skin drained all the resistance from me.

Jesus! She felt so damn good.

"I'm sorry. I invaded your privacy. I didn't know it was wrong. We're a couple," she said through broken sobs.

She sounded scared, and I hated that. I never wanted Ruby to be afraid ever again. "Don't be scared," I said, my voice husky with regret. "And you *never* invade my privacy. We are a couple. This isn't about *you*. It's about *me*."

Ruby was completely naked, and was obviously ready to climb into the shower with me. My wet body had saturated hers, and we were both dripping wet.

I felt the tension start to leave her body and her backside started to melt into my front.

Nothing had ever felt so damn right.

"Then what happened just now?" she asked tearfully.

"I got scared," I confessed after I'd swallowed the lump in my throat. It was time for me to get real with her.

She'd fucking trusted me with every horrible thing that had happened in her past, so I was done being a coward.

"Why were you afraid?"

"Because the lower half of my body is uglier than what you've seen on the top," I rasped against her ear.

Something about Ruby always made me spill my guts, even when I didn't want to.

She started to squirm so hard in my hold that she got turned around and nailed me with a glare I'd never seen before.

"Are you trying to tell me that all this is over something that is completely superficial?" she asked in a furious tone.

I locked eyes with her, and what I saw coming back at me was pure anger. It was the first time I'd ever seen Ruby really pissed off, and her fury was mesmerizing.

"You don't know how bad it really is," I told her roughly.

"Seriously?" she shrieked as she pushed on my chest. "Well, let me see this awful sight for myself. Get back in the shower."

"Ruby, I'm not—"

"This isn't about *you* now," she said in an unforgiving voice. "It's all about me and whether I'm as superficial as the bitch who dumped you. And whether or not my delicate self can handle what happened to you."

I had no idea what had happened to the sweet Ruby I adored, but this incensed, bossy Ruby was kind of a turn-on, too.

I backed up as she gently pushed me back into the shower, and then got in herself, slamming the glass door hard enough that I hoped it didn't shatter.

She folded her arms across her chest as she surveyed every inch of my body while my back took the brunt of the water from the shower nozzle.

"What in the hell do I have to do to make you understand that I want you? That I'll *always* want you," she said desperately. "Just tell me and I'll do it. I've spent every day fantasizing how it would be if you fucked me, and I think I pretty much covered every position. I need you, but I can't make you trust me."

I felt like a dick. "I'm sorry. You don't need to do anything. You're fucking perfect, and I *do* trust you."

She'd done plenty to prove that my injuries weren't going to affect the way she felt about me. I'd just been too deeply absorbed in my own fears that I hadn't heard her.

But her message was pretty loud and clear now.

She moved forward and put her hands on my chest. I didn't breathe as she started tracing every one of my scars.

"I don't always like my body, either," she confessed. "And it took all the courage I had to show you the scars I had from my abuse. But it's something I can't change any more than you can fix your scars. They're part of us. Part of our history. But they don't have to define us if we want to move forward. Neither one of us deserved the pain we went through. But haven't we had enough pain now, Jett? Wouldn't it be better to let it go and look at our future?"

She looked up and I searched her face. The only thing I could see was the same fucking longing I was feeling. "I didn't doubt you, Ruby. I doubted myself."

"You hurt me," she said with brutal honesty.

My gut ached as I looked at the hint of sadness in her beautiful dark eyes.

"I know. I'm sorry," I answered.

She shrugged. "Shit happens. I doubt it will be the last time we'll piss each other off."

I grinned. "At least I know you're perfectly capable of standing up for yourself."

She shook her head. "That wasn't just for me. It was for you, too. Your reality isn't mine, Jett. I want you to see yourself as you really are instead of through your distorted lens. When I look at you, I see a strong, handsome man who got hurt trying to save people from death or permanent captivity and torture. You put your own well-being on the line without hesitation. And you have the scars to prove it. You're my hero, Jett. Don't you know that?"

I had to swallow the enormous lump in my throat before I could answer, "And you're mine."

Emotionally, I hadn't been in a good place when I'd met Ruby. But she'd changed me for the better when she'd crashed into my life, healing all my open emotional wounds that I'd gotten from the accident and my agonizing recovery.

"Can I touch you now?" she asked with a sultry expression. "I feel like I've been waiting forever."

"Yeah," I croaked.

As she dropped to her knees, I wondered what I'd just agreed to, and whether I was going to live through it.

Chapter 22

Ruby

My heart was racing like crazy as I lowered myself to my knees to touch Jett's leg.

It wasn't exactly the gnarled mess that Jett made it out to be, but it was incredibly scarred, and my heart ached for all the pain he had gone through because of his injuries.

But God, the man was otherwise gorgeous.

I traced his scars, and then ran my hands down his rock-hard abs. He hit the exercise room every single morning, and it showed. There wasn't an ounce of spare flesh on his body. He was all hard muscle and hot skin.

After a couple of years of physical therapy, Jett knew his exercise routine for his knee by heart. He did his PT and then got down to business on the rest of his body, and his routine was brutal, keeping his ripped form perfect.

I crawled behind him to finally cop a feel of his tight ass in all of its glory. I didn't feel the least bit guilty as I stroked over his hard glutes, thinking that I could bounce a quarter off his tight butt and send it into the stratosphere. I leaned forward to put my mouth on one cheek, then bit down hard.

"Jesus! Did you just bite my ass?" Jett grumbled.

I grinned up at him as I moved back in front of him. "Do you really think I was going to miss the chance?"

As my gaze rolled down his body, I finally looked directly at his cock, and it hadn't gotten any smaller over the last few minutes.

I wrapped my fist around the erect shaft, and then ran a thumb over the head. The ache in my core became more like agony.

"Stop, Ruby," Jett growled as he grabbed my wrist and then took my hands and pulled me up. "We're going to do this right."

He slammed the shower off, and then urged me to step out. He followed closely behind me.

"I didn't actually wash myself," I said breathlessly.

"Doesn't matter. I plan to get you sweaty so you'll need it again anyway."

An electric tingle shot down my spine as I thought about getting hot and sweaty with Jett.

He quickly dried himself, and then ran the towel over my body sensually, every touch stoking my need for him.

Finally, he tossed the towel to the floor and cupped my breasts in his hands, his thumbs lightly caressing my hard nipples.

"You're so fucking beautiful, Ruby," he said gruffly, and then pulled me into the attached bedroom.

My ass hit the mattress, and Jett came down beside me.

I watched him roll toward the side table to fumble for something inside.

"I'm already on birth control," I told him. "I have been since soon after I ran away. I went to the free clinics just in case something happened when I was on the streets."

He slammed the drawer closed and rolled, pulling me down on top of him. "Do you know how crazy that makes me?" he rasped. "That you could have been raped or worse out on the streets alone?"

"I wasn't," I told him, stroking his jaw to make him relax.

"But you could have been," he answered as he rolled me under him. "And I doubt I'll ever be able to take your safety lightly because of it."

I sighed and wrapped my arms around his neck. "Feel free to protect me."

I kind of loved Jett's alpha instinct to make sure I was always safe. After the life I'd lived the last six or seven years, it was comforting.

"Damn right I will," he vowed harshly right before his mouth came crashing down on mine.

The fire that was always right underneath the surface when I was with Jett exploded the moment his lips touched mine.

The feel and taste of him was addictive, and I'd been waiting way too long for my fix.

I was panting when he released my mouth and moved lower to explore my breasts. My nipples were painfully hard, so when he bit down gently, I let out a tormented moan. The pleasure/pain made my pussy flood with heat.

He went back and forth, his tongue lashing over my nipples until I felt like I was losing my mind.

"Jett, please," I gasped.

"Relax, baby," he said against my sensitive skin. "This is going to be a long ride."

Every muscle in my body was tense, and there was no way that was going to change. Not while he was tormenting me.

I let out a huff of relief as he moved lower, but my anticipation heightened as he parted my legs and moved between my thighs.

I knew he was going to taste me, just like he'd threatened to do the first time he'd made me come, but I wasn't prepared for what it would feel like when his tongue stroked over my sensitive flesh. "Oh, God," I moaned, my body responding so acutely to the sensation that I tried to pull back.

Without missing a beat, Jett cupped my ass to keep me in place while his mouth and tongue devoured me.

He licked from bottom to top, teasing my clit every time he reached the tiny bundle of nerves.

I speared my hands into his hair, trying to find something stable while my body flew out of control.

I wanted more.

I needed more.

But Jett seemed determined to merely explore.

I squirmed beneath him, not knowing exactly what I had to have, but hoping that he'd give it to me.

"Please," I cried out desperately.

His hands tightened on my ass, and he dove harder, his tongue more focused and insistent on my clit.

"Yes," I hissed as I started to climax, a sensation I was very familiar with now.

I tightened my grip on Jett's hair, realizing this orgasm was different, even more powerful than I'd experienced in the past.

Lifting my hips, I welcomed every stroke of his tongue.

My back arched as I screamed, "I can't take it, Jett."

But he showed me that I *could* and *would* take everything he had to give.

I imploded as my orgasm crashed over me, my body shaking as Jett brought me slowly down to earth.

He crawled up my body and kissed me, letting me taste myself on his lips. The embrace was sensual and hot, and I wrapped my arms around his neck and savored the feel of our heated bodies skin-to-skin.

I was consumed by a pleasant haze of lust as I was coming back down to earth that I wasn't prepared when Jett thrust his hips forward and firmly seated himself inside me.

There was some pain, but some primal need to be joined with him was so satisfied that I didn't care.

I panted as Jett remained still. "Relax, sweetheart," he said in a raspy voice near my ear. "We needed to get the bad part over quick."

"I knew it wasn't going to fit well. You're too big."

"Jesus, woman. You *are* good for my ego, but it fits. It just takes some getting used to. I think I'm exactly where I've always belonged."

I understood. Somehow, I felt like I'd always been waiting for Jett.

The pain subsided, and all I could feel was Jett stretching me, filling me. And the sensation went beyond physical. My spirit was soaring.

"It's better," I said breathlessly. "Is your knee okay?"

"I have no idea," he said, his warm breath wafting over my ear. "All I can feel right now is you."

He moved back, and our eyes met. I could see the strain of holding back on his face.

"Then fuck me, Jett. Please. The pain is gone. All I want is you."

"This might not last long," he warned. "I've wanted you for too long, and you feel way too good wrapped around my cock."

He pulled back slowly, and then buried himself again, which elicited a deep, wanton moan to escape my lips. "Jett," I said desperately, helpless to find any other words.

I didn't care how long it lasted. I just wanted the connection I felt with him to end with him coming apart like I'd done a few minutes ago.

"Tell me what to do," I whispered in his ear.

"Enjoy the ride," he rumbled.

Before I could say anything, my breath left me in a rush as Jett started to move with much more urgency.

"Yes," I babbled, wrapping my arms tighter around his neck. "Fuck me."

My encouraging words seemed to spur him on, and his thrusts became deeper and faster, more frenzied with each stroke.

I became hungry for more, and I started lifting my hips to meet every fierce plunge, my legs wrapping instinctively around his waist.

Just as he'd predicted, we were both sweating and lost in the pounding rhythm of a dance so carnal that I could hardly breathe. All I knew was the brutal hunger and incessant reaching to get to a place where my body gave me some relief.

I love you, Jett. I love you so much!

I wanted to scream those words out loud, but I didn't.

Maybe he didn't feel the same way, or maybe he did. But the last thing I wanted was for him to back away like he had when I'd seen him gloriously naked for the first time.

"I need you, Jett. Please!" The plea was accurate for the way I was feeling. I wanted to crawl inside him, wallow in him, and never come out again.

He moved, changing position and hefting his upper body up so our gazes met and clashed with a violent passion that nearly made me crumble from the intensity.

The strong muscles in his arms held him steady as he pummeled into me, and I met him stroke for stroke as I surged to meet his powerful thrusts.

My fists clawed at the bedspread, trying to keep my body grounded.

He'd moved into a position where his cock flirted with my clit, and the sensation of him pounding into me and the stimulation of the small, sensitive nub was more than I could bear at the same time.

"You're killing me!" I screamed as my climax steamrolled me.

We lost eye contact when I couldn't take anymore. I arched my back and gave myself over to the pleasure and the tension that Jett had built up inside me.

I felt my inner muscles clench around his cock, and his groan was definitely a sign that he was close.

"Fuck!" he yelled out as he continued to piston into me with longer, harder movements.

As I started to find my way back to earth, I watched Jett as he orgasmed, his head thrown back with abandon, the muscles in his neck flexing as he found his own release.

It was the most earthy, beautiful thing I'd ever watched.

He collapsed on top of me, but I welcomed his impressive body mass as I wrapped my arms around him tightly. I felt vulnerable, but I knew he was there to keep me safe.

There was no sound except our harsh, uneven attempts to take in air while we both tried to catch our breath.

He rolled onto his back, taking me with him so I was sprawled on top of his chest.

"I'm not even going to try to explain what just happened," Jett said coarsely as his breathing started to become normal again.

"If sex is always like that, then I missed out."

Jett tightened his arms around me. "It's not."

"Then I'm glad I waited for you," I murmured.

"I'm glad you did, too," he answered in a rough baritone.

As my eyes grew heavy, and my body sluggish, I fell asleep in the arms of the man I knew I couldn't live without.

And that thought really didn't frighten me anymore at all.

Chapter 23

Jett

From the moment I entered the Lawson complex the following morning in a custom power suit and tie, *everyone* was blatantly staring.

I didn't really blame them. I hadn't set foot in our offices since my accident.

But I'd woken up this morning ready to get to work with my crew in person.

Yes, I *could* handle most things from my home office, but I needed to meet with my senior people, and it was way past time I got back to leading my team from our headquarters. It was a talented group of people who deserved better leadership than I'd been giving them.

I was done hiding, and using the accident as an excuse not to face the world and my brothers…one brother in particular.

I wasn't exactly angry at Carter anymore, but I wasn't ready to bury the hatchet, either.

Carter drank too much, went through women like a person with a bad cold goes through tissues, and he didn't give a damn about the consequences of his actions.

He was reckless and had fallen into the superficial world that some of the powerfully rich in the world sunk into.

I didn't think he was *playing the game* anymore; he was *living* in it.

My eldest brother, Mason, did most of the traveling for the company, and also headed a difficult branch of technology. Mason was relentless in his attempt to dominate the world.

I had one brother who was too damn serious, and another who couldn't seem to think about anybody but himself.

I stepped into one of the many elevators available, and used my security code to get access to the executive suites.

Maybe I'd done fine at home. My work had always gotten done by the deadline. But I *was* the owner of one of the most powerful tech companies in the world, and we were still growing. I had an incredible team, and we were always better together.

My self-made isolation wasn't normal for me. I *liked* being with people, and I loved the work I did. I loved the comradery I felt at Lawson, and I fucking belonged here.

I'd spent just about every waking moment here before my accident, and I'd never regretted it. I'd thrived on it.

I had Ruby to thank for bringing me out of a bad place, and I was going to show her my appreciation by becoming the man I used to be.

No fear.

No hiding.

No thinking of myself as less than because I had some scars.

I used to be a cocky bastard. Maybe I'd learned a little humility, but being a hermit inside my condo just didn't feel right anymore.

"Good morning, Mr. Lawson," Shirley said from her desk as I entered.

"Good morning," I answered with a smile. "I want to see the files on the Brenner project as soon as you can get them to me."

"Yes, sir," she answered. "Would you like me to get you some coffee?"

A couple of years ago, I would have sent her running to the local coffee shop to bring me something strong and black. Now, it seemed pretty ridiculous to waste her valuable skills and make her the coffee woman.

"I'll grab some in the breakroom. I'd rather have the files."

"I can certainly do both, Mr. Lawson."

I shook my head. "No need," I answered and then headed toward the room that was usually set up with bagels and mediocre donuts along with regular coffee.

I filled a larger cup, snatched a sad-looking donut and strode to my office.

It hadn't changed.

Shirley kept everything neatly organized, and the space had been professionally decorated.

But as I sat down at my desk, I noticed that there wasn't a single personal thing in sight.

My employees loved to fill up their walls and other spaces with pictures of their families: the people who made their lives worthwhile.

In mine, there was nothing. And I had a hell of a lot bigger space than any of my employees.

I made a note to myself that I wanted to personalize my space.

"Here you are, Mr. Lawson," Shirley said as she put a large file on the desk in front of me. "Can I get you anything else?"

"Can you set up a meeting this afternoon with the entire tech team for me?"

"Of course," she answered immediately. "And can I say that it's good to have you back in the office again, sir."

I looked up at her and grinned. "You can say it. But do you mean it?"

"I don't understand." She sounded confused, which didn't happen often with my executive assistant. Shirley was pretty well-known for her calm demeanor even when shit was hitting the fan.

"Am I a good boss? I'm not asking for compliments here, Shirley, but things changed after my accident. I was wondering if there are things I can do to improve the working conditions here."

She looked relieved. "Not a thing."

"I was kind of a dick. Making you run around to fetch my coffee, and go out of your way if I wanted something different for lunch."

"That's part of my job, Mr. Lawson. I'm here to make your life easier so you can focus on what's important. I never minded doing those things because you were always appreciative. Every member of your staff respects you. And that's unusual when it comes to large corporations."

"In that case, can you possibly get me a coffee? The brew in the breakroom tastes like shit." I held out my coffee cup and winked at her. "And I think we should have Ruby provide the morning pastries. Although I might never get anybody out of the breakroom if I do."

She took the almost full coffee cup from me and dumped it out at the sink across the room as she said, "I wondered how long it was going to take for you to figure out how bad it was. I bring my own every morning."

"I think we're all coffee snobs," I observed. "We have too many excellent options here."

Shirley tossed the empty cup in the trash. "And I'm always willing to explore those options for you," she said matter-of-factly. "I usually get my second cup while I'm there in the coffee shop getting yours."

"Then I guess it works out well for both of us," I answered.

"It does," she said with a smile. "Would you like me to arrange for Ruby to deliver pastries?"

"Naw. I can talk to her when I get home."

"She's still staying with you?"

I nodded. "She's actually agreed to take me on permanently."

"You're getting married?" she asked with surprise.

"We're not quite there yet," I said thoughtfully.

"She seemed like a lovely woman when I met her," Shirley said sincerely.

"She is," I shared.

"I didn't know she was a pastry chef."

"She's not just a pastry chef. She's *the* pastry chef. Ruby is providing pastries for Indulgent Brews."

"They're the best in the city, in my opinion," she answered.

"In *a lot* of peoples' opinions," I corrected. "Ruby isn't formally trained, but her stuff is incredible. Most of her skills come from experience and creativity. She's like a pastry guru."

"Then I'd *definitely* like to call her," Shirley said jokingly. "Your services here have been sliding, and are getting worse every week."

"I'll talk her into doing some stuff up for us. I never thought about it, but if everybody is in agreement, I could contract her to work with us and get rid of the bad donut guy."

Shirley raised a brow. "You do realize that even if she doesn't have a shop, word will get around, and everybody will be clamoring for her sweets."

I raised an eyebrow back at her. I hadn't realized that my assistant was so knowledgeable about launching new products. "I hadn't really thought about it, but I think it's an excellent plan."

"Agreed," she stated. "Bring on the pastries. If they're good, they'll sell themselves."

"Thanks, Shirley."

I opened the file as soon as my assistant left the room, only to be interrupted by a voice I was hoping I *wouldn't* hear today.

"You're here. What are you doing here?"

I looked up again and watched my brother, Carter, seat himself in a chair close to my desk.

On the surface, he looked like any other businessman. Dressed in a custom suit, and without a single hair out of place, he appeared as though he was perfectly capable of taking on the entire world.

But I could see the brother I knew underneath the façade, and Carter wasn't faring well.

"To answer your question, I believe I own a third of this business. I'm back in the offices to finally move on with my life."

"Can you do that?" Carter said in a cutting tone. "Because if I remember right, that wasn't going all that well. You've been pretty much holed up at home since the accident."

"I'm recovered," I snapped. "And I don't need *you* to remind me how difficult that was."

The bastard had added to my problems instead of helping me with them.

"I heard you're seeing somebody," Carter said.

"It's none of your business *what* I do."

Carter stood. "Don't do this to yourself, bro. I checked her out. She's nobody. A homeless woman off the streets. She'll take your money and run."

I stood up. I was furious, and I was done listening to Carter's bullshit. None of what he'd said had hit home *except* his statement about Ruby being nobody.

Maybe he didn't know her, but Ruby was a way better person than Carter would ever be.

I'd talked to my eldest brother, Mason, a few times over the last few weeks, and I assumed he'd told Carter about Ruby.

I couldn't blame Mason since I hadn't said that he needed to keep the information quiet, and I wasn't about to say that.

I was proud of Ruby, and I pretty much didn't care who knew it.

"Leave," I said through gritted teeth. "Get the fuck out of my office before I kick your ass."

"No offense, bro, but I just don't see that happening," he shot back at me.

Bastard! Does he think I can't take him out because I have a bum leg?

My temper suddenly snapped, and I moved forward to teach my brother the lesson I should have given him a long time ago.

Chapter 24

Ruby

I sighed as I covered the casserole I was making with shredded
cheese, and then put it back in the oven.

It had been a busy day.

Once Jett had left for the office, I'd sourced the products I needed
to make a full range of pastries, and then went out to get them
purchased.

Then, I'd decided it was time for me to open a checking account, so
I'd stopped into the bank and took a reasonable amount of money out
of my ridiculous savings account and established a checking account.

Since I wasn't going to get paid very quickly for doing pastries, and
I knew I needed new clothes to go with Jett to his sister's wedding, I'd
caved in and decided to use some serious money from my account. I
didn't want to go to Rocky Springs looking like a homeless woman.
I wanted to look like Jett's girlfriend.

I'd spent most of the afternoon trying to find appropriate outfits for
Colorado in the fall. And I found some good prices with Pete's help.
Seattle was a bit overwhelming at times, but I was slowly getting
used to the different areas.

I just wasn't ready to get into the traffic with a brand-new BMW quite yet.

As I walked across the kitchen, I noticed the same sore muscles that had been screaming at me all day. But they still put a smile on my face.

For a guy who claimed to be encumbered by injury, Jett certainly wasn't lacking in stamina or endurance. We'd woken up a couple of times during the night just to experience the pleasure of being together all over again.

Unfortunately, I was paying for my sexual gluttony with aching muscles I hadn't even known existed.

But I wouldn't have traded last night for *any* amount of discomfort.

It had been...perfect.

I'd been somewhat surprised when Jett had gotten dressed in a gorgeous suit and went off to his offices this morning. But I'd somehow sensed that it was some kind of turning point for Jett, and I hadn't questioned him after I'd seen the grim determination on his face.

He'd seemed...different. Not in a bad way, but in a I'm-fucking-taking-back-my-life sort of way.

And it looked pretty damn hot on him.

I grabbed a potholder to pull French bread out of the bottom oven.

I was pretty much doing my lazy recipes since I'd gotten home late. Jett was getting a casserole I'd thrown together quickly, the bread I'd just pulled from the oven, and I'd whipped up some easy lemon bars as soon as I'd gotten home.

Not that I thought Jett would know the difference between a difficult pastry and an easy one that could be done in fifteen minutes. Pretty much everything sweet worked for him.

I heard the front door close, and my heart skittered because I knew Jett was home.

He was in the kitchen in less than thirty seconds, and he looked just as hot as he had this morning.

But there was one difference.

"What happened to your face?" I asked as I gently touched the bruise under his eye that *hadn't* been there when he'd left in the morning.

He didn't answer until he'd given me a kiss. "My brother's fist collided with my face," he answered gruffly.

"Your brother hit you? Why?"

I knew there was some kind of distance between the Lawson siblings. But I didn't understand why.

"We had an old score to settle. So I settled it."

"What happened?" I asked softly, hoping he'd confide in me. I wanted to understand his family dynamics, but he rarely talked about anybody except his sisters. "Why don't you get along with your brothers?"

"Mason and I get along fine," he said as he took his jacket off and tossed it over the back of a kitchen chair. "But Mason is rarely around, and he works too damn much. Something happened to my family when my parents were killed. We just all seemed to scatter. Harper and Dani went off to do their own things, and Mason, Carter, and I decided to work together. We sold off most of our parents' assets to divide up the inheritance, but we kept my dad's fledgling tech business so we could make it our own since we were all educated in technology. Everything happened pretty fast once we moved the company to Seattle and it really took off. We each have our own division, so pretty much all we ever did was work. We fell into a relationship that was more about being business partners than brothers."

He grabbed a beer out of the fridge, popped it open, and sat down at the kitchen table.

I took a seat across from him. "Were you close as children?"

"Yeah, that's the weird part. We were all pretty tight. Harper and Dani were close, and Mason, Carter, and I were like best friends. We did everything together."

"Your parents' deaths had to have been traumatic for all of you. Don't you think that sometimes those things either draw you together or tear you apart?"

I had no idea what it was like to have siblings. I was just trying to understand through my own experience of losing my parents.

He nodded and took a slug of his beer. "Unfortunately, it didn't draw us closer together. I think we were all so raw that we couldn't talk about it, so we didn't. And we didn't talk about anything else, either. Somehow, we just completely lost our family, and it went on for so long that we couldn't seem to get it back again."

"I'm so sorry," I said softly. "But it's not too late."

"It might be," he contradicted in a solemn tone. "I just wish I had noticed years ago, after our folks died. I guess we just got so caught up into becoming a leader in the tech industry that I never stopped to see how dysfunctional my family had become. And it wasn't like we needed the money. We were filthy rich before the company started its rise to the top because of my parents. But it wasn't really about the money. I guess we were caught up in the challenge. We're all hardheaded. Even my sisters."

"It's part of who you are," I told him. "And that's not always a bad thing."

Jett *was* stubborn, but that's one of the qualities he'd needed to get through his injuries.

"I'd really like it if we could reconnect. But I have no idea how to rebuild a family. Harper and Dani will be in Colorado, but it's not difficult for any of us to see each other. It's a fairly short jet ride."

"I'm glad you'll be seeing your sisters soon at the wedding."

"Maybe we could go a few days early," he suggested. "It might give me time to talk to my sisters and figure out where in the hell we fucked up."

"I'm ready when you are," I offered. "I can make my last delivery to Indulgent Brews near the end of the week and I'm free."

He grinned, and he looked like a naughty schoolboy with his black eye. "I have another job for you."

"What?"

"Can you supply breakfast pastries for my staff? They'd all worship you. We have a contract with a bakery for morning stuff, but the quality is crap for what we pay them."

"You know I'm always happy to help."

He shook his head. "Nope. This isn't something you're doing for free. Like I said, we *already pay* a bakery to provide stuff. You'd be paid accordingly. We can try it out with my office, and if it goes well, you'll get the rest of the offices, too."

I folded my arms across my chest and gave him a skeptical stare. "You're not setting this up to help me make a small fortune?"

"Absolutely not. The idea came up when I was talking to Shirley about how bad the bakery items are. Even I couldn't eat the donuts. They were stale."

I cracked a smile. "Okay. Since you never meet something sweet that you don't love, then maybe you really do need something different."

"My staff needs something better," he corrected.

"I think it's pretty nice that you actually offer the service to your staff. Most companies don't."

"It's mostly selfish," he answered. "We get more work out of them if they aren't thinking about lunch because they didn't have time to get anything in the morning."

I laughed. "You know that's not why you do it."

He shrugged. "Maybe not the *only* reason, but studies show that it ups productivity."

"I'll do some stuff tomorrow."

I ran some ideas by him for items he might want, but I could see that he was distracted.

Finally, I said, "You never did tell me what you fought about with Carter?"

"Like I said, it was an old score."

"What?" I pressed.

"He slept with my ex-fiancé," Jett said flatly.

I was speechless, unable to ask all of the questions I had that were screaming through my brain as I saw the grim expression on Jett's handsome face.

Chapter 25

Ruby

"I already know I want you to sign on to make me stuff permanently as soon as possible," Lia said as she stood behind the empty glass case at Indulgent that had been full of pastries earlier that morning.

"I second that wholeheartedly," Zeke said from a table where he was finishing off the selection of sweets she'd saved for him when I'd laid them out earlier.

With Jett seated across from Zeke, helping him devour everything, I knew it wouldn't be long before all the pastries were gone.

The two men had never met before today, but I was pretty sure they were male bonding over brownies.

"My offices come first," Jett insisted. "My employees would revolt if Ruby doesn't bake for us anymore."

I smiled because I knew what he said was probably true. I'd had the chance to chat with some of the people who worked for him, and heard the horror stories about what the bakery had been bringing their way. To me, it seemed almost ridiculous to lose the business of one of the biggest corporations in the world, but the bakery itself was growing, so they'd lost their personal touch. Their profit had obviously become more important than customer satisfaction, which I knew could eventually be their downfall.

"Once Stuart and I are married, I'm expanding and opening another store," Lia explained. "I want to start off with your products at the other store from the day we open."

"If I take on Jett's whole company, I'm going to need to get a kitchen and some employees. I'm going to have to have more ovens and space," I told her.

"Just don't open a store," Lia said. "Well, unless you *want* to open a bakery. That was kind of selfish because I'd love to have customers wanting your pastries so they come to my shop. I kind of like you exclusive."

I smiled at her. "I'm not looking in that direction right now. And please don't tell me that you won't have people pouring through the door for your coffee regardless of whether or not you carry my stuff."

It was late and the shop was closed, but it had been a madhouse just an hour earlier when it was open.

"When are you opening your other store?" I asked.

"As soon as I get my grandmother's inheritance," she explained. "She put in a weird requirement that I have to be married by the age of twenty-eight before I could inherit. I think she was worried about me becoming an old maid because there weren't any prospects in sight when she passed away."

"They can actually do that?" I said, astonished that somebody could dictate Lia's life for money.

She sighed. "Apparently, yes, she could. My attorney says I could contest it, but chances are I could lose since my grandma specified alternate places to put the money should I not meet her terms. But it's simple, right? I just make sure to get the deed done before my birthday."

"When is your birthday?"

"Next month," she answered. "A few days after I get married."

"Aren't you cutting it pretty close?"

Lia shrugged. "It doesn't matter since the wedding is already planned." She stooped down as she said, "Which reminds me that I have an invite for you and your hot guy over there."

I took the invitation from her hand. It seemed I was going to have more than one wedding to attend in the near future. "I'd love to come," I replied.

"Honestly, if I'd known about you sooner, I would have asked you to do the cake, but Stuart is anal. Everything was worked out months ago."

"That's okay," I said hurriedly. "I don't have a ton of experience doing huge cakes alone."

Lia nodded. "Honestly, sometimes I just want the wedding to be over. It's consumed so much of my time, and I've been wanting to jump on Indulgent's popularity by getting another store for a while now. Zeke deserves to get paid back for the enormous risk he took in being my partner, too."

"He's not going to be your partner anymore?"

She shook her head, and her eyes grew sad. "We were never meant to be permanent partners. It was a loan for him. Zeke and I have known each other since we were teenagers. He did it just because we're friends. And he's pulled his weight, even though he didn't have to. He helped every step of the way."

"Does he really need the money back?"

Lia pulled a face. "Oh, God, no. He isn't as wealthy as Jett by any means, but he's still filthy rich. But I *want* to pay him back. We aren't related or involved in any way, and he stuck his neck out for me. But I guess anybody who is ambitious needs a hand when the money isn't there."

I thought about her comment for a moment. "I know what you mean," I told her a few minutes later. "It was hard for me to take loans and gifts from Jett, especially when I knew I couldn't pay him back anytime soon."

"Your honey has more money than God," Lia replied. "And he's your guy. Why would you worry about that?"

"The same reason you worry about paying Zeke back."

"But Zeke and I aren't involved. And if he really wanted to give me a BMW and I knew he'd never miss the money, I'd probably take it because we're friends."

"I barely knew Jett," I confessed. "I was homeless and the victim of human trafficking. Jett saved my life."

Lia looked stunned as she answered, "Oh, honey. I'm so sorry. Were you hurt?"

"Long story. I'm okay, but do you have any idea what it's like to suddenly step into a fairy tale when you've lived most of your life as a prisoner of your circumstances?"

"Like Cinderella," Lia said in an awed tone.

I nodded. "Pretty much. Jett is almost too good to be true. Sometimes I'm afraid that I'll wake up and discover all of this is a dream."

"I get that," Lia said. "But Jett adores you. It's pretty obvious. And I doubt there's anyone in the world who deserves a happy ending as much as you do. Take what he's offering you if you want it, Ruby. I've learned not to question some things in life. Good and bad things happen. It's how we handle those good and bad times that matter."

"But he buys me extravagant stuff."

"It's only a luxury in *your world*. Think about it, Ruby. Jett has never known a day when he wasn't incredibly wealthy. It was a way of life for him even before Lawson really became a tech giant. If you think about it, Jett giving you a car is like you giving me a new pair of shoes or something. Those things are inconsequential to him, but it's a very big deal to you. So you can just give him a kiss, thank him, and move on after he gives you another car or a new mansion." She hesitated before she added, "Shit, I can't believe I just said that."

I laughed because the look on her face was priceless.

"No, you're right," I admitted. "His net worth is so enormous that it really is nothing for him. I guess that's just so hard for me to accept."

"If you're going to be with one of the richest men in world, you really will have to accept that a huge gift to you is a little thing for him. He doesn't know anything else. But I could live with making that kind of adjustment. Stuart is a millionaire, and even *that* feels uncomfortable sometimes. I didn't grow up in that world, either."

"Did he give you a new car?" I questioned curiously.

She rolled her eyes. "I wish."

Honestly, I was starting to think that Stuart wasn't the guy for Lia. After watching the way Zeke's eyes seemed to follow her around a room, I had to wonder if my new friend was marrying the wrong guy.

But no, it *had* to be my overactive imagination. Lia didn't seem like the type of woman to choose the wrong man.

"I'll try to get used to it," I said unhappily.

Lia shot me a mischievous smile. "There's a lot worse things you could have to adjust to than enormous wealth."

"I'm in counseling," I shared. "But I guess I'm still trying to accept that I'm worthy of a man like Jett."

"Hey, stop that!" Lia exclaimed. "Don't base who you are on money. It's all irrelevant when you're talking about a relationship. Nobody is *worthy* of having a fortune. It just happens. What makes Jett a good man is that he cares what's going on with people who are less fortunate than he is. Has he ever treated you like you're beneath him because of your circumstances?"

"Never," I said emphatically.

"And I already know Lawson is incredibly philanthropic when it comes to local and world issues."

"Jett does things that never make the news, too. He doesn't give to get attention. He does it because he...cares."

Lia crossed her arms. "I swear, if you don't snap that man up and just enjoy your life, I'm going to break up with Stuart and marry Jett myself."

I giggled because her statement was so over-the-top. "I am enjoying him. A lot, actually."

Jett and I had pretty much had sex on every surface in his condo, and it seemed like every experience was better than the one before.

"I won't touch that comment," Lia said with a laugh. "It could go one of several ways if I do, and they're all a little scary. But don't let money get in the way of your happiness, Ruby. It's just something that buys *things*. And none of those things can truly make you happy."

"I know. Maybe I'm just nervous because we're getting ready to take off for Colorado to attend Jett's sister's wedding. That's a whole lot of billionaires to handle at one time," I told her in a joking tone.

"None of them are any different than you," Lia assured me.

"Jett's sister is wonderful," I said. "I've met her. She's the one who sent Jett to get me out of a bad situation in Miami. She's one of the reasons I'm not homeless anymore."

"Don't be nervous, Ruby," Lia said sincerely. "You're a wonderful, intelligent, and strong woman who has some incredible talents. Don't ever let anybody intimidate you into thinking that you're anything else."

A lump formed in my throat. I knew that I needed to internalize my self-worth, and I was working on it. But it helped to start making friends like Lia. "Thank you."

I saw the guys get up from their table across the room.

"I think everything has been consumed," Lia said with humor in her voice.

"Knowing Jett, it was gone a long time ago and they've just been trading stories."

"How do two guys look that gorgeous when both of them can easily consume a ton of high-calorie stuff? Don't get me wrong, I love to eat, but it shows on my hips or my butt almost immediately," Lia bemoaned.

"Jett works out every day," I shared.

"Zeke loves sports, and he's really active, but still, it's just not right."

I laughed. Personally, I'd never had a problem with my weight, and when I was homeless, I'd gotten too thin from lack of available food. But sooner or later, I was going to have to watch what I ate or I'd be piling on pounds with all the baking I was going to be doing. Right now, I felt like I was making up for lost time, but my body was filling out pretty quickly.

Lia and I started talking business, and worked out the details of a daily menu with some things left open so I could create whatever seemed appropriate for her store that day and keep new and different things coming in all the time.

"I can have my legal department do the contract so you don't have to pay to get it done," Jett offered.

"Thanks," Lia answered. "I'd appreciate that."

"Have fun at the wedding," Lia said to me as Jett and I got ready to leave.

I nodded. "I'm looking forward to *your* wedding, too."

Jett looked at Lia, and then at Zeke. "Is that happening soon?" he asked.

"Next month," I informed him. "We just got an invitation today."

Because I knew Jett, I could see that he was troubled, but he said, "We'll definitely be there."

We had left the building and were waiting to cross the street before he commented. "I think she's marrying the wrong guy," he said gruffly. "Zeke is crazy about her."

"Did he tell you that?" I asked with surprise.

"Hell, no. He didn't tell me. But it's pretty damn obvious to me. He looks at Lia like I look at you."

My heart skipped a beat. Jett just came out and said things sometimes that touched me pretty profoundly.

It was one of so many reasons why I loved him so damn much.

Chapter 26

Ruby

"This might sound weird to both of you, but what in the hell happened to our family?" Jett asked his two sisters, Dani and Harper, as all four of us sat together in the living room of the vacation home Jett had rented in Rocky Springs, Colorado.

I'd really wanted to back away so Jett could have a heart-to-heart with his sisters alone, but he'd asked me to stay, so I remained silent, sitting next to him on the couch.

Jett *needed* to have this conversation with all his family. Unfortunately, neither of his brothers had shown up yet, so he'd decided to talk to his sisters first.

We'd been in Rocky Springs for a couple of days, and I couldn't ask for nicer people to hang out with than the Colters and Jett's sisters. Everybody had been so welcoming, and Harper and Dani had included me in everything they were doing.

The more I conversed on a grown-up level with people, the more comfortable I became. I was realizing I wasn't at all anti-social. In fact, I was just the opposite. I'd just never had much opportunity to learn adult social skills.

"It's not weird," Dani told Jett. "Harper and I have been trying to figure it out, too. It's like our family dissolved because Mom and Dad weren't there anymore to keep us together. But we were all so close. I don't know how we drifted apart."

"It actually makes more sense for you two," Jett mused. "You and Harper weren't *physically* together, and didn't see us in Seattle very much. But Carter, Mason, and I were in the *same city*, working the same damn business. And we didn't stay close. We pretty much only see each other at business meetings. It's like we were so obsessed with building on our momentum with Lawson Technologies that we forgot to be family. And none of us really had a personal life because we were working all the time."

"I think all of us handled Mom and Dad's deaths differently," Harper said thoughtfully. "Instead of pulling together to deal with it, we all tried to cover up our pain with distractions or obsessions."

"I want it to be different," Jett informed them sadly. "But I'm not sure how to fix it."

"I think we *all* want our family back again," Dani told Jett in a gentle tone. "It's not that we don't all love each other. I think we just need to move on and learn how to be a family without Mom and Dad. They've been gone for a long time."

"I still miss them," Harper said with a sigh. "But I know that the last thing both of them would have wanted is for their kids to stop being a family because they're gone. If anything, they'd want us to pull together."

Dani nodded, her eyes bright with tears. "I miss them, too. I'm sure I always will. But I miss my brothers, too."

I tried to fight back my own tears as I watched Jett, Harper, and Dani talk about how they could mend the breach that had happened in their family.

Honestly, I was absolutely no help to them because I didn't even know what it was like to have a real family, and I was an only child.

But it didn't keep me from hurting right along with the three of them because they'd all lost something they cared about so much.

Jett needed this, even though I knew it wasn't easy for him to confront. His accident had brought about a lot of challenges and sadness for him. I sensed that he needed closure on some things to be completely whole again.

Since he'd gone back to his office, I'd watched his self-confidence rise, and he seemed pretty comfortable in his own skin—or maybe I should say his custom power suits.

Jett's orthopedic doctor had finally given him clearance to return to all normal activities—of course he didn't know that Jett already had. Jett knew he wasn't ever going to run any marathons, but he seemed to accept his limitations better every day.

Jett rose to his feet as his sisters came barreling toward him from their chairs.

I brushed back a few tears as I watched his face as he caught each of his sisters with a powerful arm, holding them close with an expression of both relief and joy on his face.

Once they were all seated again, Dani said excitedly, "So catch us up on everything. When did you and Ruby realize that you wanted to be together?"

Jett answered. "Pretty much from the time she put me in the hospital," he joked.

"What?" Dani said with alarm.

Jett held up a hand. "Long story, and both of us were okay. But it happened pretty quickly."

I remained silent as he recounted the way we met, and what had happened afterward while we were in Miami.

"Why didn't you tell Marcus?" Dani asked. "Or me?"

"Because I wasn't ready," Jett stated. "However much I wanted us to be together from the moment I saw her, Ruby had a lot of things to work out, and so did I."

"A lot of it was me," I informed them in a guilty voice. "I didn't want to be a charity case to him. And I didn't want him to assume that I just wanted his money."

The women nodded their heads like they understood, while Jett grumbled, "I hate it when you say that, Ruby."

"I know. But it's true."

"So how are you doing now?" Harper asked. "I can only imagine what it was like to be all alone on the streets. And you did it for years."

"I'm doing good," I answered them with a smile. "I'm in counseling, and I'm taking things one day at a time."

"She's doing great," Jett corrected. "And she's starting her own pastry business in Seattle that I'm already certain will be a success because I'm her personal taste tester," he said playfully. "I've sampled the goods, and they're honestly unlike anything I've ever had."

"Oh, my God. Are you really a pastry chef?" Dani asked excitedly. "Mine just backed out on the cake and the desserts for the wedding, and we're scrambling to find somebody. Marcus's mom can help, but she can't make the wedding cake. Can you do it for me?"

"Dani, I've never been professionally trained."

"Does it matter if you're great at what you do?" she questioned. "If Jett says you're good, then I know you are. And we don't exactly have somebody who can handle the job here in Rocky Springs. It's a resort, not a wedding destination. Most of the businesses cater to tourists."

"I just don't want to disappoint you," I confessed.

Really, I knew I could handle doing the cake. I think it was time for me to stop denying that I wasn't *capable* of making things because I hadn't had the schooling. I'd been under the tutelage of an incredible pastry chef for years, even though I'd been young at the time. And I'd soaked up everything she'd ever taught me and now I'd even added my own twist.

Maybe I didn't know the business part of being a pastry chef, but I sure as hell could bake just about anything Dani wanted, even a huge wedding cake. My mother and I had done plenty of them.

"Please, Ruby," Dani cajoled.

I wanted to repay her kindness to me. And this seemed so small compared to what she'd done for me.

I nodded. "I can do it. Did you do a tasting? Did you decide on the flavors you want?"

"We did," she said excitedly. "Or actually, Harper and I did. Marcus said he didn't care what kind of cake I got as long as I liked it. My husband-to-be likes to pretend that he doesn't like sweets, but he actually loves them. I don't think he really has a favorite. He pretty much swipes any kind of ice cream I have."

"Do you have a bigger kitchen I can use? I can let you try my version of your flavors and see if you're okay with them. Or we could even try a few varieties you haven't tried."

"Do we have time to do it?" Dani said excitedly. "You can help yourself to the catering kitchen at Mom's resort."

I grinned at Dani and Harper. "Then we're in business. I can start early in the morning and have some stuff ready for you to try by the afternoon. My mother owned a catering business back in Ohio. I'm used to working under pressure. In fact, I'm pretty sure I thrive on it."

I never felt better than when I was juggling multiple projects around in a kitchen. For some reason, I loved to experience creativity in the middle of chaos.

"You're on. But Ruby, I'd like to pay you," Dani ventured carefully.

"Absolutely not," I answered firmly. "Dani, you saved my life. And even though this will *never* repay what you did for me, I'd like you to let me do this for you as a token of my gratitude. And as a friend who wants to give you a wedding gift."

Tears were flowing down her cheeks as she replied tearfully, "As a friend, I accept, but only because I know you have a boyfriend who's loaded. You don't owe me any gratitude, Ruby. You're an incredible woman. You've faced some pretty shitty odds, and still come out on top. I don't know the whole story, but what I do know makes me proud to have you as my friend."

Her words touched me, and I felt a door open in my soul.

I didn't have to be loaded with money or things to see myself as a good person anymore.

I could accept my talent as something special and not something that I needed to explain.

I deserved friends who would treat me with respect.

And I could love Jett for exactly what he was…an extraordinary guy who just happened to be one of the richest men in the world.

"Thank you," I answered after a few moments of hesitation. "That means a lot to me."

Dani stood, and the rest of us got to our feet. "Is she pretty solvent right now?" she asked Jett. "Because if she is, Harper and I are going shopping, and we're going to help her pick the perfect dress for the wedding."

"I have some things," I objected.

Harper shot me a smile. "Unless it's something that's ridiculously indulgent, and brand-new, we're on our way to Denver."

"It's not new," I admitted. I'd planned on wearing the dress that I'd bought when I'd done my first makeover. "But it's fine."

"*Fine* isn't going to cut it, sister," Dani said as she punched my arm playfully. "Jett is going to be in a tux because he's in the wedding. You need something amazingly sexy."

Strangely, that idea appealed to me a lot.

"Nothing too sexy," Jett grumbled. "I don't like other guys checking her out."

"Caveman much?" Harper teased.

Dani wriggled her eyebrows at me. "Don't worry. Harper and I have a couple of Neanderthals ourselves."

I laughed as Harper and Dani grabbed my hands and started to pull me toward the door.

"Wait!" Jett demanded.

We all hesitated while he strode over and gave me a toe-curling kiss, and then said, "Don't let these two get you into trouble. If you need more money, just text me and I'll make a transfer."

"I have almost two million dollars in my accounts," I gasped. "Nobody can spend that much money in one day."

He caught my chin and tipped my head up. Our eyes met for a moment and my stomach actually fluttered at the intensity of his gaze.

"Have fun," he said strongly. "I don't care how much money you spend."

"Okay," I said, shooting him a smile that I hoped expressed just how much I appreciated having a man like him in my life.

His sisters urged me out of the house after I'd quickly grabbed my purse and a pair of comfortable shoes I was pretty sure I was going to need to keep up.

Chapter 27

Ruby

"I wish I could help you," Jett said unhappily as he watched me race from one side of the kitchen to the other.

Even though the hummingbird cake that Dani had chosen was something I was familiar with, I'd started the day before with making the layers consisting of bananas, coconut, pecans, pineapple, and cinnamon.

Luckily, Dani was having a relatively small crowd with only family and friends, but that still made up around a hundred guests since Marcus and Dani had both grown up here in Rocky Springs.

So she'd decided on three layers since she and Marcus weren't into saving the top layer, which was a good thing in my opinion. No matter how hard anybody tried, year-old frozen wedding cake just wasn't palatable with *any type* of preservation.

Probably by billionaire standards, the cake was ridiculously simple. The rich and famous generally went overboard to make their cake look spectacular. Fortunately, Dani was all about how it tasted instead of making a statement. And I was determined to make it spectacular with delicious, edible things I could design over the buttercream frosting.

I looked at Jett, who was lounging against one of the cupboards. "I have it under control," I reassured him.

"Never doubted it," he shot back. "But I'm feeling a little useless."

"You're keeping me company, and getting me fed," I reminded him.

He'd brought me lunch while I was working, and had insisted that I sit down to eat it.

"It wasn't really difficult to order from the restaurant and give you the plate," he said drily. "And it's not a sacrifice to keep you company. I always want to be wherever you are."

My heart tripped like it always did when he said something sweet. "It helps," I told him.

"Then I guess I have to be okay with being a slacker," he said with a grin.

God, I loved this man who got joy out of the simple things—like just being with me. I felt the same way, but I could never just blurt things out like Jett was capable of doing.

"I think we're looking good," I said as I examined the round table on wheels in front of me.

"Are you kidding? It looks fucking amazing," Jett argued.

The cascade of flowers that I was doing down the front were almost completed, so I really only needed to do the detail work and decorate the table around the cake for presentation.

"Do you want to try it?" I asked as I shot him an impish smile.

"I think Dani would kill me," he said, sounding disappointed.

"No she won't," I disagreed, and then went to the refrigerator to pull out a small layer cake.

Jett's eyes lit up. "You made a small one?"

"I made some extra batter and frosting."

"Bring it, woman. I've been salivating over this cake all day."

I snagged two plates, a knife, and a couple of forks on my way over to the counter.

Jett dug in the second his piece hit his plate, and his eyes almost rolled back in his head as he savored it. "Jesus, Ruby! It's fucking fantastic."

I ate more slowly. "It's a Southern favorite, but my mother loved making it. I was glad Dani decided to go with it. It turns out really moist."

"Everybody will be trying to steal you away from me," he said grumpily.

I laughed. "Just because of my baking talents?" I teased.

He shook his head. "No. Your skill would be just one huge bonus, but it's enough to push any guy over the edge."

I blew off his silliness when I said, "Dani and Marcus look so happy together. All of the Colter couples do."

"They are," he agreed. "And Dani and Marcus were always meant to be together. It just never happened. It's been a long time coming."

"Were they childhood sweethearts?" I asked curiously.

"Nope. They hated each other. But I think they fought because they didn't quite know what to make of the way they felt. Marcus and Dani are complete opposites, so on the surface, they don't make sense at all. My best friend was a workaholic. He kind of reminds me of Mason. And Dani was a crazy risk-taker who rarely thought much about her safety."

"Opposites attract?"

"In their case, yes. But it took a long time for those two hardheads to figure everything out."

"I'm glad she's going to be happy."

"I'm glad she and Harper have figured out where they belong," he added.

"Maybe you can all have a relationship now?" I hinted.

"Hell, Harper and Dani have already worked out a schedule to get us together during the year, so we'll see them a lot."

"I'm glad," I said. "I really like both of them."

"They like you, too," he shared, and then went silent for a moment before he added, "My brothers will probably be more complicated."

"I'm sure they will," I agreed. How could things *not* be complicated when your brother slept with the woman you planned on marrying?

Honestly, I doubted I could ever like Carter, but he was Jett's brother, so whatever happened was his decision to make.

He didn't offer anything more, so I polished off my cake and said, "I better get back to work. This masterpiece needs to be done today."

The wedding was taking place in the afternoon tomorrow, and the reception was following here at the resort.

"Hey," Jett said as he caught my arm.

I turned to look at him, and saw the sadness in his eyes. I waited for him to speak. There was obviously bad blood between the two younger brothers, but Jett hadn't gone beyond just telling me that Lisette and Carter had been intimate.

"There's some things I'm just not ready to talk about. It's not that I don't want to, but I need to work it out for myself first."

I moved forward and put my arms around his neck. "You don't *ever* have to explain yourself to me," I told him. "Just know that I'll be here when you want to talk."

He wrapped a powerful arm around my waist and kissed me until I was just a little dizzy with delight when he let me go and gave me a playful smack on the ass.

"Back to work, woman. I want to take you home," he said in a wicked voice that I'd come to love so much.

"Then I'm all over getting this job done," I squeaked.

"I'd much rather you be all over *me*," he said huskily.

I finished the cake quicker than I'd planned. I was anticipating a very good night.

Chapter 28

Ruby

The wedding ceremony for Marcus Colter and Danica Lawson was probably the most beautiful thing I'd ever experienced. They'd made their own vows, breaking away from traditions, but the pastor still officiated the ceremony. It was unique, just like the two people getting married.

I looked down at the cake that had been carefully brought into the ballroom of the resort where the reception was now in full swing. I rearranged a few things that really didn't require moving, wanting everything to look perfect for the couple who'd be here soon to cut it.

Jett had gone off to find Mason, who had been a late arrival right before the wedding had started. So I was just admiring the gorgeous venue and all the people who were there in the room.

The cake was officially ready, and I was proud of how it had turned out.

My hand went up to grasp my necklace, just like it had about a hundred times during the afternoon. Then it moved to my earrings, checking them before I dropped my hand again.

I knew I had to relax about the value of the sapphire set of jewelry I was wearing, a gift that Jett had just given me before we'd left for the wedding. But it was hard when I knew they were probably worth a small fortune.

Not that I didn't love the necklace and earrings dripping with sapphires. Jett had chosen them because they were my birthstone, but it was slightly nerve-racking to be wearing something that probably was worth more than the BMW Jett had purchased for me.

Relax and pretend they're fake.

In theory, it was a good idea. But my brain couldn't seem to forget they were very, very real.

While I'd been in Denver with Dani and Harper, I'd purchased some inexpensive earrings while I was there. But nothing had prepared me for Jett's gift.

The sapphire set was beautiful, and I'd cried all over him for being so considerate.

Relax and enjoy them!

I straightened my spine and remembered that they were just *things.*

I was grateful that I'd gotten a completely extravagant dress for the wedding, along with a bunch of other utterly decadent pieces to add to my wardrobe.

I was pretty sure my gift from Jett would have looked totally wrong with the dress I'd brought with me from Seattle, so I was glad I'd shelled out some money to get something a lot nicer. And sexier.

The black evening dress that Jett's sisters had talked me into was, in their words, *sexy enough to make a man beg, but not sexy enough to be trashy.*

I smiled as I remembered the pained expression on Jett's face when he'd seen the dress. The cut-out back and the hem that landed just above my knees had been a little bit too much for him, even though it was actually pretty tame compared to some of the others I'd seen.

The dress had been worth every penny when I saw the heat of desire in his eyes when he'd looked at me.

"How much money would it take to get you out of Jett's life?" a low baritone asked smoothly from behind me, jolting me out of my thoughts.

I turned sharply, almost colliding with the large form that was now in front of me.

It was Jett's brother, Carter. I hadn't formally met him yet, but I'd seen him at the ceremony.

My first impression was that he was aesthetically very pleasing to look at, but his blue eyes were as cold as a glacier. Dark-haired like Jett, he also had some of his younger brother's features, but he lacked any animation. Carter was as cold as Jett was warm. Everything, down to the smallest detail, was absolutely perfect. He looked at home in a tuxedo, like a male model who was taught to put on a sophisticated demeanor. But nothing about Carter seemed to be an act. I could almost feel the chill as I looked back at him.

"Excuse me?" I said politely, certain I'd heard him wrong because of the noise in the venue.

"You heard me," he answered grimly, as though he'd read my mind.

"Why would I *want* to get out of Jett's life?"

"I want to know how much money it will take to get you out of my brother's life," he rasped. "I want you gone, never to communicate with my brother again. How much? I'm willing to make giving up your sugar daddy worth it."

"He's *not* my sugar daddy," I answered, getting irritated by Carter's presumptions. "You know nothing about me."

He lifted an arrogant brow. "On the contrary," he said bitterly. "I know everything I need to know. You were homeless, and Jett loves to pick up strays. He gave you a place to stay, and because he was an easy mark, you manipulated everything you could from him. So far, I know he purchased you a new vehicle, and those pretty blue sapphires you're wearing right now. I have no idea how much cash he's laid out because I can't get to his bank records, but I'm assuming he set you up well with money, too. Jett is nine years older than you, and he has limitations because of his accident, not to mention

the fact that he's severely scarred. But I suppose you can overlook
those things when he's giving you everything you want. Must look
pretty good to you. The only thing you have to do is sleep with him.
And I have a feeling that's not a problem since I assume you were a
prostitute when you met him."

"I was *not* a hooker," I denied angrily, folding my arms in a defen-
sive act that helped me feel stronger.

Truth was, Carter Lawson was probably the most intimidating
man I'd ever met, as well as one of the meanest. And I was feeling
slightly vulnerable.

"Interesting," he observed. "Too bad I have a hard time believing that."

"I don't give a damn what you believe," I retorted.

"I can put a million dollars in your bank account tomorrow," he
said with nothing but steely determination in his voice.

"Your brother was a lot more generous," I said, my voice dripping
with sarcasm. "He put in two million."

"Five million," he countered.

*Did this man really think he could buy people's actions? Did he
really imagine that if he didn't like somebody, he could just pay to
make them disappear?*

"I don't want your money," I said sharply.

"Then what do you want, Ruby?" he drawled, his tone skeptical.
"What will it take to get your claws out of my brother? Do you really
want to be stuck with a man who can't keep up with you because he
has physical limitations?"

Tears started to pour down my cheeks, but they were tears of
sorrow. They were proof of the fury and frustration I was experiencing, and I was done listening to this man say negative things about
a man he couldn't possibly even understand or appreciate.

"Jett *has no limitations*," I snarled. "And I'm with him because I
love him. You'll never be even half the man your brother is, with or
without his money. And you sure as hell shouldn't be finding fault
with anyone else when you slept with your own brother's fiancée.
You're despicable."

Before I could think, I lashed out and slapped him across the face, sending the drink in his hand flying and snapping his head to one side.

The satisfying sound of my hand connecting with his face was enough to not make me regret what I'd done.

He reacted immediately, his hand reaching out to grab my arm.

People were staring now, but I was too emotionally riled up to care. "Don't touch me. Don't *ever* touch me," I hissed as I yanked and pulled myself free. "Money doesn't make you less of an asshole. It just makes you a *more powerful* asshole to people who care about your status. I don't. Just like your brother, I judge people by their actions and not their net worth. And just for the record, Jett is *eight* years older than me, you jerk."

I turned around and ran, stumbling a little as I tried to see through the flood of tears that were flowing down my face.

"Bastard!" I said as I moved through bodies to get out of the building so I could compose myself.

In some ways, I had to admit that my relationship with Jett was unlikely, and looking at us from the outside, it wouldn't be hard to make the wrong assumption.

Homeless girl who was on the streets and hungry.

Rich guy who had a good heart.

I'd never really thought about how the situation looked before, but now I couldn't help but wonder how many other people had made the same conclusion as Carter.

Chapter 29

Jett

"Give me one good reason not to put your ass in the hospital," I growled as I grabbed my brother, Carter, and pushed him up against the nearest wall.

I'd seen red the minute I spotted my brother putting his hands on my woman from across the room, and that color had filled my vision as I saw Ruby trying to get away, obviously upset and crying.

Nobody touched Ruby. Not ever.

"I didn't hurt her," he said hostilely as he pushed me back and freed himself from the choke hold I had him in. "Jesus, Jett! Are you really going to do this to yourself again? How many users are you going to go through before you learn your lesson?"

"She's not using me, shithead," I said vehemently. "She probably could have, but she didn't."

I moved toward him again, but I felt a strong hand on the neck of my tuxedo holding me back.

"Don't, Jett," a masculine voice said. "This is our sister's wedding. Don't make a scene."

Mason.

His comment was the only thing that held me back, but as my eldest brother slowly let go of me, I knew I didn't want this for Marcus's and Dani's wedding. I'd flatten Carter somewhere else. But not here.

"What did you say to her?" I asked angrily, my brother Mason moving forward to stand next to me.

Carter shrugged. "I was trying to buy her off. You don't really want her, Jett. For God's sake, she was a homeless prostitute before you took her in."

I moved forward again instinctively, but Mason had a restraining hand on my tux again before I could get to Carter.

"She wasn't a prostitute," I informed him. "She was a virgin. Ruby was a teenage runaway who had every reason to leave home. When I met her, she'd been kidnapped by a human trafficking ring and they were ready to sell her to the highest bidder. Anything that's ever happened to Ruby was *not* her fault. And she's been through hell. She's taken very little from me, even though I offered her everything. She's strong, and she's a survivor. But she's not a user. She's starting her own business, and she's doing very well without my help." I took a ragged breath in before I continued. "I offered to marry her, and she refused because she didn't feel like she had enough to give me in return. That is not my idea of a woman who wants to use me."

"Doesn't sound like it to me, either," Mason confirmed.

I shrugged out of Mason's hold. "I need to go find her. I'll deal with you later," I told Carter in a warning voice and turned around to go find Ruby.

It gutted me to think that one of my own family members had made her feel small, and may have hurt her.

But I'd make it right. I had to.

I was obsessed with my beautiful girl who looked at me like no other guy existed.

As I walked away to go find my woman, I wondered how anybody could ever think that Ruby was the lucky one when I knew damn well it was the opposite.

My dark-eyed angel had stumbled into my life just when I'd needed her most, and I knew I wasn't going to survive without her.

Carter could go fuck himself.

"Do you really love him?"

I was surprised by the baritone voice that spoke from the darkness, and I stopped the swing I was riding on, even though I knew exactly who had spoken.

It was Carter Lawson, the last person I wanted to talk to at the moment.

When I'd run away, my only objective had been to escape after I'd left the ballroom, pretty sure nobody would find me on the playground that sat some distance away from the main resort. I'd stumbled upon it by accident. I'd stayed because it seemed like a good place to think. "How did you find me?" I asked him coldly.

Carter moved up beside me and sat in the swing next to me as he answered wryly, "I have two sisters. Why is it that women always want to go stare at the moon and stars when they're pissed off, anyway?"

The only illumination nearby was a tiny solar light near the merry-go-round, so I couldn't see much of Carter except his massive form next to me, but it seemed pretty strange that a guy like him, dressed in a tux, would be sitting on a large swing set. "I don't know," I answered with a sigh. "And yes, I love him. How could I not? Your brother is the most amazing man I've ever known."

The anger I'd felt toward Carter was gone, but my hurt about what many people probably thought about my relationship with Jett was still bothering me. Maybe Jett didn't care what people were saying, but the last thing I wanted was to be a source of gossip for him.

"I never really slept with Lisette," he said. "I only told Jett that I did because I knew she was going to be poisonous for him after his accident. For weeks, she put off coming up to the hospital. But

I knew she'd show up eventually, and that he'd be crushed because Lisette had no heart. She's always been a bitch, but he never really saw it. I wanted him to dump her, and since he believes in marriage, I thought the one thing that would get him to break up with her was if she was cheating."

"So she never came to see him at all? Not even when he was critical?"

"Not once," Carter confirmed. "She was too busy with her social life."

"Oh, God," I said, shocked that a woman could be engaged to a guy and not rush to the hospital when he was in bad shape. It was almost unfathomable. "Why haven't you told him the truth?"

"I tried. I swear I did. But he wouldn't listen. The sad part of the drama is that he'd already seen Lisette earlier in the day, and she'd broken up with him. She was with him for the first and only time, when he was still in a lot of pain, just to break up with him. But I blurted out my lie before he could mention that he was already free of her claws. So I lost my brother for nothing."

I didn't have siblings, so I had no idea how much Carter had risked to tell Jett something like that. But I could imagine it hadn't been easy. "You were trying to manipulate him when he was down," I admonished.

"For his own good," Carter rasped.

"For what *you thought* was good for him," I corrected. "Jett was a grown adult. He should have been allowed to make that choice for himself."

"Maybe," he agreed. "But it's not easy to watch somebody you love making a big mistake. He would have been miserable with her. And she was going to make his recovery more difficult. I was trying to do the right thing."

"But you're wrong about *me*," I informed him. "I don't care about your brother because of his money. I love him because there isn't another man like him on the planet. I'm sorry you can't see how incredible he is, but I see it."

"I'm starting to think maybe you really do," Carter said stoically.

"Jett has risked his life for other people, and he's done it a lot. He sees things that other people ignore, and he tries to do everything he can for others. He isn't a self-centered jerk."

"Like me?" he asked drily.

"I'm not going to answer that question because you probably wouldn't like the answer," I snapped.

"So I guess upping my offer wouldn't work?" he questioned carefully.

"No." Carter was such a jerk, but I sensed he wasn't really trying to get me out of Jett's life anymore. "If I thought I wasn't good for Jett, I'd leave with *nothing* in a heartbeat. But I never considered the fact that people might gossip about him having a homeless woman as a girlfriend. I hate that."

"What happened to make you leave home as a teenager?" Carter asked. "Jett didn't really say."

It touched me that Jett had kept my secrets, but I was tired of being ashamed of a past I had no control over. I was finally recognizing the fact that I'd been given one life as a child that I didn't deserve, but I'd be damned if I was just going to lay down and accept it as a grown adult.

I was in control now.

I didn't have to be afraid or let it taint my entire adult life.

"I was molested and abused. When my parents died in an accident, I went into the full-time custody of my abuser. He tried to rape me, so I ran away. Please don't ask me anything more. That's all I really want to share with you," I said firmly.

Since Carter was Jett's brother, I wanted to give him some insight into my broken soul, but I knew I needed to decide just how much I wanted to share. Little by little, because of my counseling, I was learning to set my boundaries.

"I respect that," Carter agreed. "But it's fucked up. Our parents died in an accident, too, but we all had plenty of money and each other, and we were all over eighteen."

"Imagine if you didn't," I said softly. "Just think about how it would be if you'd had to figure out where to go, how to eat, how to get to a place where you could sleep. That was pretty much what consumed me every single day for well over five years. And until I turned eighteen, I was paralyzed by the fear of getting taken back to my abuser."

"I'm sorry," Carter said hoarsely. "Who did you say abused you?"

"I didn't."

"Do you want to tell me so I can kill the bastard?" he said.

I exploded with a surprised laugh. "No. And he's already dead. Jett went looking for him, but he had a heart attack several months ago and died. What's with the Lawsons and their desire to commit murder?"

"None of us can stand bullies," Carter answered.

I found that amusing since Carter was probably the biggest bully I'd ever met, but he obviously had his own idea of what a bully really was, and who fit that mold.

I changed the subject. "Are you going to tell Jett that you didn't really sleep with his girlfriend? It definitely wasn't the right thing to do, but I think he'd be relieved that you didn't really do it, and were only trying to help him in your own misguided way."

"If he'll stop beating the crap out of me long enough to listen."

"You can't control other peoples' lives, Carter, even if you're trying to help."

"You have no idea what it was like to watch my brother suffer after the accident," he rasped.

"But he's okay now," I said reasonably. "Why were you trying to buy me off?"

"He's *not* okay, Ruby," he said forcefully. "He's never going to be okay again. You didn't know Jett before his accident. He was an expert skier, basketball player, and he could kick my ass at almost any sport. He's never going to be able to do that again."

I kicked my swing into motion while I thought about his words. "You feel guilty because you can do those things and he can't," I finally concluded.

"Hell, yes, I feel guilty. Marcus approached me about PRO, too, and I should have been there with Jett, but I was too obsessed with our world domination to get involved. Maybe I could have protected Jett if I'd been there."

"And maybe you couldn't have," I pointed out. "It was a tragic accident, Carter. Jett chose to be there. And if you'd talk to him, I think you'd understand that he's pretty okay with himself as he is right now. He knows he can't do everything he used to do, but he's happy."

"Because of you," Carter said morosely. "And I almost screwed that up, too. Now that I see the whole picture, I understand that he's changed. He isn't hiding at home anymore. I could see that things were different from the moment he walked back into the offices again. But I've gotten overprotective. Maybe I was even holding him back, and trying to talk him out of anything that I thought would hurt him."

"You don't need to do that anymore," I said simply.

"I get it," he agreed.

"In a lot of ways, Jett and I are healing each other," I said, just now realizing that my assumption was true. "Jett was a little broken when we met, and I was a train wreck."

"I guess a brother isn't always the best person to make a guy realize that their life isn't over," Carter replied.

"You weren't feeling his pain like somebody who is broken can," I explained. "Jett and I understood each other because we were both trying to recover from something that seemed like it was impossible to forget."

"Ruby?" Jett's voice called out.

"Here," Carter called back.

I looked up to see a dark form coming toward us.

My heaviness in my chest disappeared as Jett reached for me and pulled me into his arms.

"Get lost, Carter," Jett demanded. "And if you ever get near Ruby again, I'll do a hell of a lot more than punch you," he growled.

Carter stood. "I was trying to make shit right," he grumbled.

I could see Jett's face now, and I put my fingers over his lips as I said, "He's telling the truth. Carter didn't hurt me. We were just talking."

"I don't give a shit," Jett muttered angrily. "I still want him somewhere far away."

"I'm leaving," Carter said. "But you're going to have to talk to me someday."

"Not today," Jett answered in a cranky tone.

I saw Carter walk toward the lights of the resort as I hugged Jett tightly. The two brothers would need to make their peace. I knew that now. Maybe Carter had been extremely misguided, but he'd obviously done the stupid things he'd done because he cared about his younger brother. And he'd never completely betrayed Jett. Now that I'd met him, I doubted he was even capable of those actions.

Whatever his faults, Carter Lawson was loyal to his brother, even if he was a jerk.

Chapter 30

Ruby

Jett's arms tightened around me as he said, "Don't ever do that again, Ruby. Don't ever fucking walk away."

"I wasn't leaving *you*," I explained. "I was leaving the situation."

"Don't do it again," he demanded a second time. "It scared the shit out of me when I couldn't find you. Let's head back to the house."

"I'm okay now," I argued.

"I'm not," he replied in a voice that was vibrating with emotion. "If I don't get inside you right now, I'm going to lose my mind."

My heart and my body fired at the same time, and I pressed against him to try to stop the ache that was pulsating inside me. "Then maybe you shouldn't wait," I said in a sultry tone I barely recognized.

"Don't screw with me right now, Ruby, or you might get more than you're asking for," he said gruffly right before his mouth captured mine.

My hands threaded into his hair, my breath taken away by the hunger in his kiss. I opened to him and gave back as much as he gave, feeling the same insatiable desire I always did to climb inside him.

I couldn't get close enough, even though I fought desperately to try to absorb him into every cell I possessed.

I moaned as he cupped my ass and pulled me hard against his cock, but it only fueled the flames more.

I gasped for breath as he let go of my lips. "I love you," I blurted out as I panted. "I don't care if you don't feel the same way. I can't keep it inside anymore."

My heart was racing, but I felt relieved to finally say the words. I'd been holding back a volcano of emotions, and they'd finally erupted. All that love had to go somewhere, and it was now pouring all over the man who was the source of the explosive pressure.

Jett froze as he questioned, "What did you say?"

"I love you. I love you so much that it physically makes my chest hurt." I wasn't about to back down and pretend I didn't say it.

I was over not being completely honest. I was okay with myself, and even though I'd probably always have some issues from my past, I was done letting my uncle control me.

I was all grown up and I was in love with Jett Lawson.

"Fuck!" he cursed as he finally moved and put his forehead against mine. "Don't say that shit to me if you don't mean it, because you'll never get away from me, Ruby."

"I mean it," I replied without hesitation. "And I have no desire to go anywhere."

"Then how can you even question whether or not I feel the same way?" he said in a graveled voice as he tugged me over to the merry-go-round, sat down on the metal surface and pulled me down on top of him.

"Do you?" I asked as I straddled him, the metal cold against my legs.

With his hands gripping my ass to support my body and keep it from tumbling from his lap and onto the dirt, he replied, "I've been completely screwed since the first time you looked at me like you wanted to trust me, but you couldn't. I've never really believed in love at first sight, but I knew we belonged together from that very moment, Ruby. And that love just got deeper and more intense with every moment we've spent together since. Now I can't live without you anymore. And I was hoping to hell that you'd stay with me forever or I knew I'd be completely fucked."

I remembered the first time we'd locked eyes up on the auction stage. For an instant, I'd felt something, too. But I'd been too terrified to trust my initial instincts. "And the marriage proposal?"

"I already knew you belonged with me," he growled. "And I never wanted anybody touching you again. But the last thing I wanted was to scare the hell out of you. So I figured I'd settle for whatever I could get."

My heart was still so full that I wanted to cry. I lowered my head and gave him a gentle kiss. "You should never *settle*, Jett. You deserve *everything*."

"I have it," he grunted. "Everything that means something to me is right here on this playground. I love you, Ruby. Maybe I didn't understand what love could be before, but I get it now, and I fucking worship you."

He stroked a hand up and down my back. I sighed and leaned into him. "You don't always have to worship me," I advised. I didn't mind getting down and dirty whenever he wanted. "I just want you to *love* me."

"Already do," he grumbled.

I ground my hips down, staying there for a moment to enjoy the feeling of his hard cock riding against my panties. "Then let's talk about that urgent need you have to get inside me," I insisted.

"Ruby." He groaned as he tried to make me stop humping him. "I'm not taking you outside in the cold on a goddamn playground."

It had been a beautiful day for a wedding, and it was unseasonably warm for fall. Marcus had been teasing his bride that the weather didn't dare be anything other than perfect on their wedding day.

After dark, it had cooled down, but it wasn't exactly freezing.

"I'm an Ohio girl who knows what cold really is," I said as I reached between our bodies to liberate his cock. "And you'll warm me up."

I'd been aching for Jett from the moment I'd heard his voice, and I wasn't taking *no* for an answer. "I need you," I whispered into his ear.

"Then I'm giving us both what we want," he growled.

"I want you," I confessed with a sigh.

He stood up and took me with him, letting my feet slowly find the ground.

He placed my hands on the bars of the merry-go-round and bent me over. "Don't move," he demanded.

I shivered, his tone so commanding that I wasn't about to argue.

In less than a minute, Jett was lifting my little black dress, lowering my panties and caressing the cheeks of my ass. I gripped the metal bar harder as he moved a hand between my thighs.

The first stroke of his fingers over the sensitive flesh of my pussy nearly made my legs give. "Oh, God. Jett, please don't tease me," I gasped.

"I'll show you as much mercy as you had for me, sweetheart," he answered, his voice heavy with need.

I knew I was going to pay for poking the beast, but I didn't care.

I gasped as Jett tormented my clit, his rhythmic strokes strong, and without his usual finesse.

When he impaled me with his cock, I arched my back with satisfaction and pressed back against him.

Both of us were raw and hungry, desperate to get what we needed. And anything except giving each other everything wasn't going to satisfy us.

Our joining was frantic and chaotic. It felt strange to be completely dressed, but so intimately connected.

I was so submerged in satiating the need that was clawing at me relentlessly that I didn't notice anything except the feel of Jett surging forward and filling me over and over again.

Jett's tight grip on my hips was the only thing that kept me grounded as he pummeled into me.

"Come for me, Ruby," he demanded. "I'm not going to be able to hold back."

I could sense his tension, and I knew everything was way too intense and urgent this time. Without thinking about what to do, I acted on instinct, lifting my hand and putting it between my legs to rub the tiny bundle of nerves that I knew would set me off.

"Hell, yes. Help me this time, baby," Jett growled.

My fingers slid into my warmth and wetness that felt like silk, and I felt my climax rushing up to meet me almost immediately.

"Jett," I screamed, slightly terrified by the magnitude of the force rushing up to meet me as my orgasm hit me hard.

I grabbed onto the bar again with both hands as I rode a wave of pleasure that was ferociously taking my body over.

"Ruby!" I heard him groan as he held onto my hips and buried his cock one more time.

I would have collapsed if Jett hadn't been there with a pair of strong arms that held me tight as I milked him to his own heated release.

I couldn't move as I tried to recover my breath, and my body was still trembling as Jett cleaned me up, presumably with his own handkerchief, and then pulled my panties back onto my ass.

My theory was confirmed when he turned me around just in time to see him slide the hankie back into his pocket.

I stepped forward as his arms wrapped around me, and my head dropped to his shoulder.

"I can't believe we just had a quickie on a playground like a couple of horny teenagers," Jett said hoarsely as he nuzzled my neck.

I smiled at his words. "Are you complaining?" I asked. "I know I'm not."

"I'm not exactly complaining, but I don't think I'm always comfortable with the way I feel about you. You make me crazy," he confided.

I wrapped my arms around his neck and kissed him, letting him know that I felt exactly the same way.

Chapter 31

Ruby

"They look so happy," I said to Jett as we watched the bride and groom share a dance.

I'd talked Jett into going back to the reception. There was no way I wanted him to leave when he was the best man, and the bride was his sister. Not because of me.

My body was still singing after our activities in the dark, and my heart was so full of love that I could hardly breathe.

I'd briefly wondered if anybody had seen us, but it would have been difficult since we'd been so far away and there was very little light. But even if they had, I couldn't regret it. And I'd noticed that Jett had positioned our bodies so his back was to the resort. Even when we got crazy, he was *always* protecting me.

"Marcus has no idea what he just signed up for," Mason said from his position next to us at the table.

"None," Jett agreed.

"Dani's a wonderful woman," I told Jett as I slapped him playfully on the shoulder. "Marcus is a lucky guy."

"She's a handful," Mason observed. "You have no idea how much trouble she got herself into when she was a kid."

"Marcus is screwed," Jett answered with humor in his voice.

"Both of you stop," Harper insisted from across the table with Blake at her side.

Strangely, both of the guys went quiet, and I saw Blake smirking as he looked over at Mason and Jett.

It was amusing to see two super-rich guys stop talking the minute their sister scolded them.

Carter was noticeably absent, but I'd told Jett the whole story that his older brother had shared with me, hopeful that he'd eventually forgive and forget. Even though Jett was angry that Carter had tried to control his life, I thought that I'd heard a note of relief as Jett was grumbling about Carter stepping too far over the line.

As I looked around the table, I told myself I'd do everything I could for the man I loved to get his broken family back together.

They needed each other, even though some of them still probably didn't want to admit it.

"The cake is fantastic, Ruby," Harper said as she set her fork down on her empty plate.

I opened my mouth to tell her that it wasn't bad for a non-professional, but I shut it again. I was done critiquing everything I did. So I just said, "Thank you."

"You're learning," Jett said in a low voice next to my ear.

I smiled at him. "Yes, I think that I am."

"And the cake *was* fantastic," he said with a grin.

"Have you ever met a cake you didn't like?" I asked with a delighted laugh.

"Not that I can remember," he answered. "But I happened to love yours."

My heart did a happy dance as I realized that we were talking about more than cake. "I love you," I whispered quietly.

"I love you, too, baby," he said, not bothering to lower his voice. "And I don't give a damn who knows it."

"I don't care, either," I confessed. "I'll get on the table and announce to everybody here that I love you, but I guess I just kind of want to keep it all to myself for tonight."

"No getting on tables," he warned. "Every guy here could see up your dress."

"You're impossible," I told him.

"You're beautiful," he replied.

My body infused with a warmth that had nothing to do with sex and everything to do with the fact that Jett Lawson loved me. Sometimes he said outrageous things, but I knew he meant every one that he uttered.

"My Cinderella story isn't over," I said softly as I watched the bride and groom take the floor again for a slow song. "When I'm here with you, and I look at this ballroom, it feels kind of surreal. Not long ago I was homeless, and now I'm all dressed up like a person just going about a regular life. Okay, maybe not *regular*. More like *extraordinary*."

"It's finally how it was supposed to be," Jett concluded.

"I'd do it all over again if I'd still end up with you," I told him.

"Not happening," he argued as he wrapped a possessive arm around my waist. "You don't need to do it all over again. I already have an ulcer from thinking about something happening to you."

I sighed. I had no idea how I'd gotten from one place to another so fast, but I wasn't going to question fate.

I slowly rose to my feet. "Will you dance with me, Jett?" I asked as I put a hand on his broad shoulder.

I held my breath as he gave me a startled look. "Ruby, you know that I can't—

"We'll take it slow," I said, feeling several pairs of eyes on us as I encouraged him to do the very thing that his ex-fiancée said he'd never be able to do again.

Both of us had grown so much, and I was pretty sure I knew what Jett was capable of doing.

He just wasn't so sure he knew what he could do.

"I was a lousy dancer *before* I had the accident," he warned, his voice slightly uncomfortable.

"He's lying," Harper said. "He's a fantastic dancer."

I looked at Jett's sister, giving her a look to let her know I was grateful for backup.

"But it will give you a good excuse to feel me up," I bent down and said in a whisper.

My heart lurched as I straightened up and saw genuine fear in his eyes.

Maybe I'd made a mistake.

Maybe I'd pushed him too far.

Maybe I'd hurt him.

He stood up and wrapped his arm around my waist. "You really know how to convince me to do anything. You got me with the *feeling you up* part."

I beamed up at him as I took his arm. "Good. Because there's nobody else I want to touch me but you. And I don't believe you can't dance."

I searched his face, trying to tell him with my eyes that there was nothing to stop him except himself.

"You'll find out if I end up dumping us both on our asses," he said roughly as he took my hand and led me slowly out to the floor.

I didn't give him time to think about what he was doing as I slid my arms around his neck. "I think dancing can be like making love to someone in a different way," I told him.

"I'm pretty okay with the old way," he rumbled as he took my hand and wrapped his arm around my waist.

I laughed as he led me slowly around the dance floor. It was a very slow beat, and Jett was easy to follow as I leaned into him just enough to try to make him forget that he was dancing.

I rested my head on his shoulder, and we fell naturally into a slow rhythm that was comfortable for both of us.

We swayed together until I finally said, "You're a phenomenal dancer."

"You're nuts," he said, his voice lighter. "And you lured me into this with lustful promises."

At that moment, I knew that everything was going to be okay. Jett and I were made to challenge each other, but only in the best of ways.

I felt his hand stroke across my back, and the sensation made me shiver.

"I'm sure you were born with lustful thoughts," I answered, teasing him.

"I'm only that way with you," he said huskily as he leaned back to look at me.

I fell into the emerald green of his eyes, my heart stuttering as I tumbled.

When he swooped in to kiss me, everything that had ever been wrong in my world righted itself.

I might not be completely healed, and I had no doubt that I'd still struggle with my issues for a very long time.

But tonight, my broken soul had come back together again, and I was more than happy to live with the cracks that needed time to disappear.

As long as I had the beautiful man who was holding me, there was very little I *couldn't* do.

Epilogue

Ruby

One Month Later...

"I'm glad they didn't get married," Jett said as we left the church where Stuart and Lia were supposed to get married. "She's heartbroken," I told him.

"No, she's not," Jett argued as he opened the door of the sedan and waited for me to get into the car.

Pete had parked outside the church and he looked startled when I jumped inside.

Jett explained to his friend and driver that the ceremony never happened, and we'd be headed back home.

"No woman wants to be left at the altar," I admonished.

As the car started moving, Jett said, "Better that than married to a jerk. I expect we'll get another wedding invitation pretty soon."

"From who?" I asked curiously.

"Zeke and Lia," he explained calmly. "Zeke will make his move now that Lia has to get married or lose her inheritance."

"She doesn't love Zeke," I pointed out.

"If she doesn't now, she will. Those two were meant to be together. She didn't really love *Stuart*. I think she just talked herself into loving the *idea* of being married to him."

After watching Lia as the wedding approached, I couldn't exactly say that Jett was wrong. Honestly, I didn't think Lia loved Stuart, either. "I hope she ends up with Zeke," I conceded.

It was obvious that Zeke adored Lia, and he'd treat my friend right. Unlike Stuart, who sounded like a complete jackass.

I leaned back against the leather seat and watched the city roll by as we headed back toward downtown.

The last several weeks had been busy, and I was exhausted, but in a good way.

Things had irrevocably changed between Jett and me since Dani's wedding. With all our fears out in the open, we could help each other finish healing.

I had moments when I got scared, but Jett was there to keep me grounded. In return, I tried to alleviate any issues he still had from his accident.

I talked to Harper almost every day, and Dani was due back from her honeymoon soon, so she'd be back in the loop, too.

Carter and Jett had buried the hatchet, and surprisingly, Carter had become one of my greatest supporters. He was almost like the big brother I'd never had to defend me, and he took those duties seriously.

Nothing like two alpha men to drive a woman crazy.

But honestly, I wouldn't have it any other way. I had to admit that I'd had a soft spot for Carter since I'd realized that his intentions were good. It was just his execution that had been bad.

Mason was gone again to international sites, so we hadn't seen him since Dani's wedding.

I'd been busy with the bakery stuff, so Jett had become my willing mentor, teaching me the management side of having my own business.

Everything had happened quickly after I'd started doing regular work for Lia's shop and preparing for a second Indulgent Brews. I was still supplying Jett's office, and he wanted me to take over for all the offices. It was going to be a huge job in addition to all of the other businesses that were approaching me every single day.

I'd wanted to break out.

And I thrived on being busy, but everything had been crazy the last few weeks.

I was finally going to be making a ton of money. While I loved the fact that I'd be independent, being wealthy hadn't been my goal. I'd wanted some kind of safety, and I'd wanted independence.

Now that I was accomplishing those goals, all I wanted was to be doing something I loved.

I'd received the enormous insurance settlement. It had been deposited into my account with very little fanfare, and since Jett refused to take a penny of it or to take back the money he'd deposited, very little had changed.

The car came to a halt and Jett got out and held the door open for me.

"You're quiet," he observed. "Everything okay?"

I answered when we got into the empty elevator, "I'm more than okay."

He grinned at me as he hit the button to the penthouse, and I smiled back.

Jett had brought more joy to my life than I could have ever imagined when I'd been homeless.

We entered the penthouse and Jett took my coat as he said, "I can't wait to give you something."

"No more vehicles," I cautioned.

He shook his head. "It's not another car. But it comes with a catch."

I followed as he wandered toward the kitchen. He stopped in the living room.

"What's the catch?" I asked eagerly. "Does it involve anything kinky?"

"Unfortunately not, but I could make it that way," he answered as he reached into his pocket. "Right now, it pretty much involves taking *me* if you accept it."

I had to catch my breath as he opened the red velvet box in his hand and the light caught the beautiful diamond inside. "I'm hoping this time you'll say *yes*. I love you, Ruby Kent. Marry. Me."

I had a brief flashback of the one other time he'd asked the same question. It was so familiar, but so different.

When he'd asked me the same question when we'd first met, he hadn't done it with the same adoration and fire in his gaze. But I did see a little bit of the same apprehension I'd seen back then.

"Yes!" I said immediately, my heart galloping inside my chest as I threw myself at him.

He caught me with a laugh. "If you would have given me that answer when I asked the first time, we'd be married by now."

"It wasn't right," I shared.

He moved back to put the gorgeous ring on my finger. "Maybe it wasn't, but I was willing."

I gaped at the enormous diamond for a moment before I said, "It's right because I love you."

Jett kissed the ring on my finger and then dipped down and gave me a kiss that tasted like forever.

"I was going to take you out to dinner tomorrow," he said after he lifted his head. "But when I picked up the ring this morning, all I wanted was to see it on your finger."

"I can live without dinner," I said as I stroked his cheek. "Take me to bed."

"Demanding woman," he grumbled, but I could see the desire written all over his face.

"Are you complaining again?" I teased.

"Never," he said hoarsely as he took my hand. "Just the fact that you want me as much as I want you is a fucking miracle."

I followed him as he tugged on my hand. I knew he wasn't putting himself down because I felt the same way, too.

Sometimes, love really was a surprising phenomenon that could make a person think about how lucky they were to have somebody who felt the same way.

As I followed Jett into the elevator, I realized that my Cinderella story had ended. But I was more than ready to start a new sequel.

I was going to be laughing, loving, and spending the rest of my life with my soul mate.

I already *had* a real life fairy tale, and it didn't get any better than that.

~The End~

Author's Note

Human trafficking is a form of modern-day slavery. It's a crime when a trafficker uses force, fraud or coercion to control another person for the purpose of engaging in sex acts or soliciting labor or services against his/her will.

So many runaways or throwaways (people that will probably never be missed) are recruited into prostitution this way. They're sometimes drugged and beaten into submission, or a non-existent debt is held over a victim's head to force them to cooperate until the bogus debt is paid.

If you or somebody you know is a victim or suspected victim, please call the National Human Trafficking Hotline for help.

Let's end this dehumanizing crime against humanity for good.

Please visit me at:
http://www.authorjsscott.com
http://www.facebook.com/authorjsscott

You can write to me at
jsscott_author@hotmail.com

You can also tweet
@AuthorJSScott

Please sign up for my Newsletter for updates,
new releases and exclusive excerpts.

Books by J. S. Scott:

Billionaire Obsession Series
The Billionaire's Obsession~Simon
Heart of the Billionaire
The Billionaire's Salvation
The Billionaire's Game
Billionaire Undone~Travis
Billionaire Unmasked~Jason
Mine for Christmas (Simon and Kara Short Novella)
Billionaire Untamed~Tate
Billionaire Unbound~Chloe
Billionaire Undaunted~Zane
Billionaire Unknown~Blake

Billionaire Unveiled~Marcus
Billionaire Unloved~Jett
Billionaire Unchallenged~Carter
Billionaire Unattainable~Mason
Billionaire Undercover~Hudson
Billionaire Uexpected~Jax

The British Billionaires
Tell Me You're Mine

Accidental Billionaires
Ensnared
Entangled
Enamored
Enchanted
Endeared

Sinclair Series
The Billionaire's Christmas
No Ordinary Billionaire
The Forbidden Billionaire
The Billionaire's Touch
The Billionaire's Voice
The Billionaire Takes All
The Billionaire's Secret
Only A Millionaire

The Pleasures of His Punishment

The Pleasures of His Punishment: The Complete Collection

The Billionaire Next Door

The Millionaire and the Librarian

Riding with the Cop

Secret Desires of the Counselor

In Trouble with the Boss

Rough Ride with a Cowboy

Rough Day for the Teacher

A Forfeit for a Cowboy

Just what the Doctor Ordered

Wicked Romance of a Vampire

The Curve Collection: Big Girls and Bad Boys Series

The Curve Collection: The Complete Collection

The Curve Ball

The Beast Loves Curves

Curves by Design

Writing as Lane Parker

Dearest Stalker: Part 1

Dearest Stalker: A Complete Collection

A Christmas Dream

A Valentine's Dream

Lost: A Mountain Man Rescue Romance

Made in the USA
Middletown, DE
02 September 2021